SUGAR CREEK GANG
The COLORADO
KIDNAPPING

Paul Hutchens

MOODY PUBLISHERS
CHICAGO

Original Title: *Wild Horse Canyon Mystery*

ISBN: 0-8024-7028-9

3 5 7 9 10 8 6 4 2

Printed in the United States of America

PREFACE

Hi—from a member of the Sugar Creek Gang!

It's just that I don't know which one I am. When I was good, I was Little Jim. When I did bad things—well, sometimes I was Bill Collins or even mischievous Poetry.

You see, I am the daughter of Paul Hutchens, and I spent many an hour listening to him read his manuscript as far as he had written it that particular day. I went along to the north woods of Minnesota, to Colorado, and to the various other places he would go to find something different for the Gang to do.

Now the years have passed—more than fifty, actually. My father is in heaven, but the Gang goes on. All thirty-six books are still in print and now are being updated for today's readers with input from my five children, who also span the decades from the '50s to the '70s.

The real Sugar Creek is in Indiana, and my father and his six brothers were the original Gang. But the idea of the books and their ministry were and are the Lord's. It is He who keeps the Gang going.

PAULINE HUTCHENS WILSON

1

We first learned about the mystery of Wild Horse Canyon while we were still at Sugar Creek, three days before starting for our summer vacation in the Rockies.

It was half past one, Friday afternoon. In a few minutes, just as soon as Little Jim got there, we would open our gang meeting, decide a few important things, then go in swimming. It would be our last happy-go-lucky swim until we got back, because while we were out West, we'd have to use hotel or motel pools where there'd be a lot of other people. Mountain streams would be too cold to swim in and really enjoy it.

We were all lying in the shade of the Snatzerpazooka tree, about twenty feet from the sandy beach of our swimming hole. Snatzerpazooka himself, the scarecrow we'd hung up early that summer to keep the crows from gobbling up the new shoots of corn in Dragonfly's father's cornfield, was swaying in the lazy afternoon breeze. Dragonfly's new Stetson cowboy hat was hanging on his left wooden shoulder.

Circus, our acrobat, was up in the tree. In fact, he was sitting on an overhanging branch close to the tree's trunk, using the trunk for a backrest.

Little Jim kept on not coming, and we kept

on feeling impatient, waiting for him. In a way, Little Jim was the most important member of the gang. That is, it was extra-important that he be there at this meeting. It was his folks—his township trustee father and his very musical mother—who were taking us with them on the out-West vacation. They were going to spend two weeks at a famous music festival in the mountains, and we were all getting to go along. I could hardly wait till next Monday.

Little Jim, the cutest member of the gang and maybe the most cheerful, was one of the best boys there ever was, I thought, as right that second I saw him coming along the path that leads from the spring to the Snatzerpazooka tree.

"Here he comes!" I exclaimed to the rest of us. "Hurry up!" I yelled down the narrow, weed-bordered winding path to him and expected to hear him call back cheerfully, "I'm coming!" as he nearly always does whenever anybody yells to him like that.

He came puffing up to where we were, but there wasn't any usual cute little grin on his cute little mouse-shaped face. Instead, his lips were set, and he was either sad or mad about something. I couldn't tell which.

"'S'matter?" Poetry asked him. "How come you're so late?"

Little Jim's worried, teary-voiced answer cut like a knife into my heart when he said, "It's Crescendo! Something's happened to her. We can't find her anywhere. She didn't sleep in her box last night or the night before, and she didn't come home this morning. She's been gone two whole days!"

We all knew what he meant when he said "Crescendo." He meant the very cute calico cat that had been Little Jim's pet ever since he was only five.

Little Jim was sad all right; he was also mad. He took a swipe at a tall mullein stalk with the striped walking stick he always had with him. He broke the mullein stalk, and its yellow-flowered head bent over and hung upside down.

"We wanted to give her to the animal shelter to feed and look after till we got back—and now she's gone!"

While Little Jim was getting his breath and telling us about Crescendo's being lost, strayed, or stolen, Dragonfly cut in to exclaim, "Who cares about a calico cat? Let's get started swimming!"

Big Jim growled back at him, "We're having an important meeting! Besides—don't you remember?—we have to examine the creek bottom first!"

"Why?" Dragonfly whined, pretending he didn't already know, and sneezed. In fact, he sneezed three times in rapid-fire succession—which meant we weren't starting on our mountain vacation any too soon for him. Hay fever season was already here.

"Because," Circus called down from his tree seat, "the heavy rains we've been having lately may have washed a lot of junk into the swimming hole, that's why. A waterlogged old stump, sharp rocks, or broken bottles or tin cans we might get hurt on. Or maybe the water washed out a few dangerous holes."

I knew what he was talking about. Every year after the spring floods and also after every big summer rain had sent a rush of water swirling down the creek, we tested the bottom to be sure our swimming hole was still a safe place to swim. Sometimes it wasn't until we'd taken out quite a lot of junk that had been washed in.

Anyway, while we were waiting to test the creek bottom—and also trying to cheer up Little Jim, who was really worried about his calico pet, which was one of the prettiest cats I ever saw—we decided to look over some of the out-West advertising Big Jim had brought with him. It was some he had gotten in the mail that very morning from the town near which we were going to camp for two whole weeks, high in the Rockies. We would go into town every day to a big tent in a meadow there to hear the wonderful music of some of the world's greatest musicians.

Big Jim hadn't any sooner opened the *Aspen Avalanche* than Dragonfly let out a happy exclamation, saying, "Look! There's a cowboy wearing a hat just like mine!"

What he was looking at and exclaiming about was a full-page advertisement for a rodeo that was going to be held in Aspen. Right in the middle of the page, sitting on a very pretty horse, was a man in a Western outfit, and on the man's head was a swept-brim hat, which, I noticed, *was* just like Dragonfly's. For half a second, I envied the spindle-legged little guy that his folks had let him have a big broad-brimmed Stetson while mine hadn't let *me*.

Then I saw the name of the cowboy and let out an exclamation myself. "Hey!" I cut loose with. "It's Cranberry Jones!"

Boy oh boy, oh boy oh boy! my mind exclaimed. Cranberry Jones, whose voice I'd heard on the radio and had seen different pictures of riding his famous palomino horse, was going to be one of the stars at the Aspen rodeo, and we would get to see him ourselves!

Dragonfly sprang to his cowboy-booted feet, swept his swept-brim hat from Snatzerpazooka's left shoulder, shoved it into our circle, and exclaimed, "See! His hat's just like mine!"

Poetry grunted, shrugged, and in his duck-like, squawky voice answered, "Yours is like *his*, you mean."

Dragonfly pouted back, "What's the difference? Just so they're alike!"

I looked at his chimpanzee-like face and at the hat he had just put on and liked him in spite of him.

Big Jim broke up our nonsensical argument then by saying, "Look, you guys! Want a mystery to solve while we're out there?"

Just the word "mystery" brought my mind to excited life. Big Jim had turned back to the front page, where there was a column of news items with a heading that said: "Rolling Stones from the Avalanche."

Below the heading were interesting stories of things that had happened long ago. Each had a different date. One was "Thirty Years Ago This Week." Another was "Twenty Years Ago." Another, "Ten Years Ago." And down near the bottom were a few lines about an old man named Joe Campbell, Cranberry Jones's stableman, who had died of a heart attack last New Year's morning. Joe's body was found in a snowdrift just outside the stable door only a few yards from where one of Cranberry's palominos was standing, saddled and showing evidence of having been ridden.

"Joe's habit of taking very early morning rides 'for my health,' as he always expressed it, had been the cause of his death. The weather had been just too cold for an old man to venture out." That was the way the story ended.

But the mystery that Big Jim had just pointed out had happened the night before on New Year's *Eve* and had a heading that said:

BLONDE DISAPPEARS AFTER MIDNIGHT
DRINKING SPREE IN WILD HORSE TAVERN

Circus right that second came scrambling down the tree, shaking the branch Snatzerpazooka was hanging on and knocking some of the sawdust out of his stuffed head—Snatzerpazooka's stuffed head, I mean. Some of it fell into my eyes so that for a second I couldn't see what I was seeing.

Besides, some of the print in the story was blurred and several lines were worn. Even some of the words were missing. It was a spooky story about a young lady who had come to the Winter Ski Festival. The story said, "She took a few lessons on the Little Nell Beginner's Slope, then was away to the more dangerous runs: The Cork Screw, Ruthie's Run, and even the treacherous FIS. Yesterday, after the morning mail . . ."

Big Jim, who was reading aloud to us, stopped. "Her name's worn off," he said, squinting at the paper, holding it close to his eyes and trying to make out the missing word.

"Let *me* see," Poetry said. "I've got twenty-twenty vision without glasses." He studied the story, then in his usual mischievous tone, remarked, "Like it says, she's *missing*"—which wasn't very funny.

Big Jim read on. "Yesterday after the morning mail . . . seemed despondent and spent most of the day alone. She was seen late at night at the Wild Horse Tavern bar. About midnight she left the bar and was last seen fighting her way through the blizzard toward her motel four blocks away. She did not arrive at the Snow-slide and at press time still had not been found."

Big Jim finished reading the news article to us. It was like reading the first chapter of an exciting mystery story in a magazine and seeing at the bottom of the page the words "To Be Continued."

"Look!" Circus exclaimed. "There's an editor's note!"

And there was. It began, "The mystery is still unsolved. The story has been pointed up this week by the owners of the Snow-slide, The Cranberry Jones Enterprises. Jones himself has offered a $500 reward for any information . . ."

That was as much of the editor's note as there was. The rest was worn away, maybe by the paper's being much handled in the mail.

Well, it wasn't any ordinary mystery story, and it wouldn't be continued in next week's *Avalanche*. If there was ever any new chapter, somebody would have to find the disappearing woman.

Already my mind was out there in the mountains in last winter's blinding blizzard, trying to imagine who the woman was and what had happened to her. I was wishing that when we got there we would stumble onto a clue of some kind that would help us solve the mystery.

"I know what I'll do with the five hundred dollars, if I get it," Dragonfly piped up. "I'll get me a palomino just like Cranberry Jones's. I'll—"

"If *we* solve the mystery," Poetry countered, "*we'll* divide it six ways between us, and your share'll be eighty-three dollars and thirty-three and one-third cents."

Little Jim chimed in then. "I wonder what was in her letter that made the woman so sad."

Poetry came back with another idea, which was, "When we get out there, I'll bet we'll find the missing body ourselves."

Big Jim, who had been lying on his stomach, rolled over, straightened to a sitting position, and with a puzzled expression on his face, asked, "Who said anything about a *body*? It just said the woman disappeared in a blizzard at midnight, New Year's Eve."

Poetry scowled. "But she had to have a body to disappear in, didn't she? Here, let me see the paper."

Big Jim handed him the *Avalanche,* and after Poetry had read awhile, he yawned and said to us, "Well, gang, we'll have to solve the mystery ourselves. A woman just doesn't go up in smoke or disappear into thin air!"

Big Jim must have felt a little irked at our barrel-shaped friend because he answered him, "Who said anything about thin air! She disappeared in air that was full of swirling snow!"

Poetry grinned back, looked at his wristwatch and quacked, "High altitude air is always thin." Then he added, "Time to go in swimming"—which it was.

Going in didn't seem as important as it had, though, because all our minds were probably out in the Rockies with a mystery running around in them. In less than a week we'd be out there for real, having a wonderful vacation. One of the first things I was going to do, I thought and said so, was to walk past the Wild Horse Tavern where the golden-haired woman had been drinking the night she disappeared. After we had our tent pitched away back in the mountains somewhere along Maroon Creek or maybe on the Roaring Fork, we'd all put our heads together and see if we could help solve the mystery. Maybe we could solve it, and maybe we couldn't.

2

As I watched Dragonfly carefully hang his hat on the swaying shoulder of Scarecrow Snatzerpazooka again, I couldn't help but think of Cranberry Jones and his own swept-brim hat and wonder how come he had offered $500 to anybody who could give any information about a disappeared woman who had just stayed for a-while in his motel. Maybe he knew who she was.

I quick was on my way to the sandy beach. In a minute we'd all be in.

Testing the bottom of the swimming hole to see if it was safe was part of what Scouts call their Eight Defense Plan. Big Jim, who had a Scout manual, had told us about it. Some of the rules of the Eight Defense Plan were for large groups of boys and were not needed for a gang as small as ours.

But one thing we always watched out for especially was if any of us seemed to be having any trouble such as cramps while we were in the water, which so far none of us had had. The only problem we had once in awhile was when we were having so much fun we accidentally stayed in too long, and Dragonfly or Little Jim got the shivers, and their lips turned blue. They'd have to quick leave the water and sit in the sun awhile to get warmed up.

Also, once I had done too much diving when I wasn't quite over a summer cold and had gotten an earache. My ear drained for almost a week after that—and it was my own fault. A boy shouldn't go in swimming with a full stomach or a bad cold.

"Everybody ready?" Big Jim asked then, and we all were.

Pretty soon we were in the shallow water at the edge of the bank, holding hands, making a line about ten feet long—or wide, whichever you want to say it was—and were slowly wading out toward deeper water, carefully feeling our way along the bottom with our twelve bare feet, not stepping on anything until we had first tested to see what it was.

It certainly was a wonderful afternoon. A lazy breeze was blowing, and the sun on the riffle downstream made it look like gold dancing cheerfully along, not caring whether it got anywhere or not.

Even though my mind was out in the Rockies in a blinding blizzard searching for a clue, and I was hardly aware of the gang at all or of Poetry's hand, which was holding onto mine—he was on the right end of our line—my ears couldn't help but hear the cheerful, very musical *"Oucher-la-re-e-e-eee"* of the red-winged blackbirds in the bayou behind us. At the same time, my eyes kept watching about a hundred whirligig beetles cruising around in worried circles on the water. Their flat, black oval bodies were shining and making the whole place smell like a bushel of very ripe apples, which is the way whirligig beetles smell when they're worried or excited or scared. Their bodies give off a milky fluid, which is what makes the odor—kind of like a skunk's body does when it is excited or worried or scared or angry. Except that a skunk's scent doesn't make a boy think of ripe apples but of apples that have been too ripe too long.

We hadn't waded out into the creek more than five yards when Circus's feet found something on the bottom. He quickly stooped, reached down a long arm, and brought up a whiskey bottle that was full of water. He looked at it, the jaw muscles below his ears tensing and relaxing, his face grim. I knew what he was thinking. He was thinking that whiskey and other alcoholic drinks had been his father's boss for many years and had been the cause of their family's having so many heartaches.

He was maybe remembering also that the One who had made the world had saved his father one night in a Good News Crusade, and Mr. Browne hadn't taken even one drink since.

Quick as a flash, Circus swung back his strong right arm and gave that flask a fierce throw down the shore. For a few seconds my eyes followed the bottle flashing in the sunlight, then I heard it crash as it struck a rock at the head of the riffle. That was maybe the twenty-fifth time I'd seen Circus do that to a bottle like that. Not a one of us said a word, but we were thinking.

We all caught hands again and waded on out

across the swimming hole. We'd taken only a few more slow, cautious steps when Poetry suddenly squeezed my hand three or four times to get my attention. Leaning over, he whispered, "I know what could have happened to the woman."

Just that second, Dragonfly on the opposite end of our hand-to-hand line, let out a couple of explosive sneezes and broke loose with a yell, crying, "Hey, everybody! I've found something down on the bottom! It feels like an old gunnysack with . . . with . . . with . . . *ouch!* Something bit me on the big toe!"

Dragonfly's scared yell, exploding in the middle of our safe swimming exploration of the bottom of the creek, sent us on a *splashety-sizzle* dash to where he was.

The water there was almost waist high to Dragonfly and a little more than hip high to Big Jim.

Even while Big Jim was going over to see what it was, my mind was trying to imagine what kind of wild animal with sharp teeth would be alive in a gunnysack on the bottom of our swimming hole—and why?

And how could it be *alive?*

Big Jim's feet told him Dragonfly had really discovered *something* strange down there, and in seconds he was down and up again with a sure-enough gunnysack with something in it. The neck of the sack was drawn shut and tied with several twists of binder twine wrapped round and round.

"Look!" Poetry exclaimed, puffing for breath

from the excitement and because of the fast trip he'd made from the other end of the line to where we were. "There are two bricks tied to it! That's what Dragonfly bumped into."

I'd already seen two red bricks, each the kind with a hole in the center, wired to the neck of the sack. And already I was guessing what was inside.

In a little while we had splashed our way to shore, none of us stopping until we got to the Snatzerpazooka tree, where our clothes were and where, on the old scarecrow's wooden left shoulder, Dragonfly's hat still was.

Little Jim was shaking as though he had the shivers. His fists were doubled up, and there were tears in his eyes.

Now the sack was open—and that's when Little Jim let out a heartrending cry. "That's my kitty! That's Crescendo! Somebody stole her and drowned her!" Then he broke out into the saddest crying I ever heard.

There certainly isn't anything musical about a boy's crying over a killed calico cat. Seeing Little Jim's tears and hearing his sobs woke up my temper. I could feel it getting hotter and hotter until, pretty soon maybe, it would be so hot it'd explode. I *did* ask a hot question with sizzling words, "*Who* would do it? Who would be mean enough to tie a beautiful cat in a sack, weight it with bricks, and throw it into the creek to drown?"

Even while I was asking, I thought I knew the answer. Sure. The heartless boy would have to be Shorty Long, the meanest new boy in the neighborhood.

Little Jim stooped and stared through his tears at his dead pet. He sniffled and then astonished us all by saying under his breath— not to us but to Somebody who was everywhere and whom Little Jim liked with all his heart— "Forgive them for . . . for killing Crescendo, for they don't know what they are doing!"

I knew what was in Little Jim's mind right that second—the true story of something that had happened two thousand years ago on a hill close to a cemetery. For a second my thoughts flew out across the creek and over the trees past the white clouds floating in the bluest sky, across the United States, over the Atlantic Ocean, and back through history to the time and place where the Savior had died to take away the sins of the world. I saw Him in my mind's eye, nailed to a cross, and heard with my mind's ear the people jeering and calling Him names. I could almost hear Him say in a tone of voice that would break a boy's heart to hear, "Father, forgive them; for they do not know what they are doing."

Just when I was all stirred up in my mind to want to give Shorty Long a licking within an inch of his life, Little Jim, whose cat Crescendo had been killed, was ready to forgive whoever had done it!

It seemed kind of wonderful to have a boy like that as a member of the gang.

Having a funeral for Crescendo—which we

did, burying her in her burlap bag coffin under the Little Jim Tree up in the woods— took our minds off going swimming and, for a little while, off the mystery that was waiting for us out West when we would get there sometime next week.

Maybe I'd better explain that it was Circus who suggested we bury Crescendo under the Little Jim Tree at the bottom of Bumblebee Hill. "The tree where Little Jim killed the fierce old mad mother bear and saved all our lives that time would make a good memorial for her," he suggested.

Little Jim's face brightened a little at the idea.

Most of us weren't satisfied, though. It seemed we ought to form a posse, take a fast hike to Shorty Long's house, and avenge the murder of Little Jim's very pretty pet. But he wouldn't let us.

When the funeral was over, I watched for a chance to ask him why, and this is what that wonderful little guy answered: "My mother prays every night for Shorty Long's mother that she'll be saved." With that, Little Jim took a fierce fast swipe with his walking stick at a mayapple growing all by itself about two feet away from a family of other ten-inch-high mayapple plants. The end of the stick struck the mayapple's lemon-shaped yellowish fruit, which was overripe, squashed it to smithereens, and scattered its insides all over.

We wouldn't have time to go back and go in

swimming now. We had to begin getting our suitcases packed for the early Monday morning start for the West.

We did go down to the spring, though, to get a drink of water, and that was where Poetry, watching his chance to get me alone, finished what he'd started to tell me while we were wading around in our swimming hole—before he'd been interrupted by Dragonfly's excited yell about what his feet had found.

Poetry and I stopped at the Black Widow Stump while the rest of the gang went down the incline near the leaning linden tree to the spring below. "You want to know what I've figured out happened to the woman?" he asked me in a whisper.

Of course, I wanted to know, and said so.

And this is what he answered in the mysterious tone of voice he usually uses when he is talking detective stuff. "I've been studying maps of the Aspen territory and reading the folders. She could have stumbled along through the drifts, not seeing her way, and walked right out into one of the heated motel swimming pools and drowned, and—"

I cut in on him to say, "But then they'd have found her, and there wouldn't have been any mystery."

"That's what I say," he countered. "She *could* have, but she didn't. Also, she could have hired a taxi for only ten dollars and fifty cents to drive her to Glenwood Springs, where she could have caught a train for Denver or somewhere and—"

I tried to cut in on him again, but he shushed me, holding up a forefinger to warn me the gang was on its way back up the incline. He went on. "*Or* she could have walked the four-and-a-half miles west of town on Highway 82 to the Aspen airport and hired a pilot to fly her someplace."

"In a *snowstorm?*" I exclaimed at him. "In a wild blizzard at night, when every plane would have been grounded?" I was surly in my voice and in my mind, because I'd been hoping he had really thought up something sensible as to what happened to the mystery woman.

All I had gotten out of what he had said was a little information about the place where we were going to spend our vacation. There was taxi service to Glenwood Springs, air service if you went out four-and-a-half miles into the country on Highway 82, and some of the motels had heated outdoor swimming pools.

We got a chance to find out how wrong all Poetry's ideas were when, right in the middle of our first week in the Rockies, we found a clue that sent showers of shivers up and down our spines and made our vacation one of the liveliest we'd ever had—and also one of the most important.

3

We certainly didn't expect to find our first clue while we were still hundreds of miles from where we were going to spend our vacation—and in the most unexpected place!

We camped the first night in a wooded area near a little river in a private campground the ranch owner called Lazywild. First, we set up the tent, made a fire in the outdoor fireplace, and helped Little Jim's mother get their gasoline camp stove going. Then, because the river was close by, the sun was still up, and the weather extrahot, it seemed we ought to plunge in and work up still stronger appetites by swimming and splashing around a little.

The rancher, whose name was Sam Alberson, warned us, "Take it easy out there, boys. We've had a lot of rain this summer, and there might be an old stump or two. Water was pretty high last week when that there cloudburst hit this part of the country. No use getting your shins skinned up. And I wouldn't try diving. The water's not deep enough."

As we'd done back home when we found Little Jim's calico cat in a gunnysack, we tested the bottom of the stream first. We waded all the way across and back at the place we were going to swim in, and once up and down, but didn't find anything except a couple of old tin cans. So we plunged in and had a wonderful time, getting ourselves good and hungry and a little more tired than we had been.

Almost too soon, Little Jim's mother called us to come to supper.

At the same time, Circus, who was near the shore, exclaimed, "Look at this! Somebody's been drinking here!"

I looked where he was looking and saw a quart bottle shining in the late afternoon sun. Circus quickly stooped and picked it up. *In a second,* I thought, *he'll swing back his strong, long right arm and throw the bottle as far as he can.*

That was what he'd started to do, when Dragonfly stopped him, yelling, "Don't throw that away! It's got something in it. A letter or something!"

And Dragonfly was right. Even with Little Jim's mother's voice still in my mind calling me to supper, and my own appetite pulling me toward camp, I still wanted to see what, if anything, was in the bottle Circus had found.

You could have knocked me over with a sunbeam, I was so astonished at what we found in the bottle.

When he had opened it, Circus took out a note and read it aloud.

Whoever finds this, take warning! Alcohol is ruining my life. Try as I will, I cannot get free from the bottle. Someday it will kill me. It will do the same for you if you take it into your life.

Around the campfire, while we were having hot cocoa, sandwiches, and the warmed-up spaghetti and meatballs Mom had sent along in a sealed container, we talked about the warning in the bottle and wondered who had put it there.

We had just finished eating when the rancher in whose campground we had our tent pitched came out to see if there was anything we needed. Spying the empty bottle, he shook his head and frowned. "The Devil's best friend. My father died an alcoholic, and my mother with a broken heart." He looked with a scowl toward Little Jim's father.

It took Little Jim's mother only a minute to make clear to long-mustached Sam Alberson that neither she nor her husband—and, of course, not a one of the Sugar Creek Gang—would be foolish enough to drink alcohol, which whiskey is one-half of.

"It may be useful as a preservative in medicines and as an antiseptic, but as a beverage—*no!*" Little Jim's usually mild-voiced mother had more fire in what she was saying than I'd ever heard her have. Hearing the Sugar Creek church's pianist say that in that way made me realize my parents were even more right than I had thought they were when they had taught *me* never to use alcohol as a drink. I had promised them I never would.

Circus broke in then, to say, "I found the empty bottle out there on the shore."

Sam Alberson's attitude changed quickly at

Little Jim's mother's answer and Circus's explanation. "There was a sad case here some time ago because of this stuff. A young woman rented one of the cabins for a week—for her health, she said. She spent a lot of time writing and reading, hiking up and down the creek, and she rented one of our saddle horses every day. I didn't know then that she was an alcoholic, because the first week she didn't drink at all. But her second week was one long binge. She stopped swimming and boating and riding and just lay around camp."

Big Sam Alberson shook his head sadly, looking around the fire at all of us. Then he cleared his throat. The sound in the dark was a little like a bullfrog's *"Grum-m-m-mph."* Then he finished, "Such a beautiful woman! Her whole life ruined. I wonder what became of her."

Because we all wanted to be up early in the morning, break camp, and get going toward the Rockies, we quick had a short devotional time around the fire, and with the last words of Little Jim's father's prayer in my mind, I was in the tent with Circus and Poetry getting ready to undress and slip into my sleeping bag.

Circus was going to keep the whiskey bottle for a souvenir of our trip, and he had the note that had been in it in his shirt pocket.

"Let me see it a minute, will you?" Poetry asked Circus, who handed it over. "Care if I keep it for you in my wallet?"

The note tucked in his wallet, Poetry whispered to me to come outside a minute. He had something to tell me, he said. What he told me was, "I've an idea. Let's slip down to the camp office and get a bottle of pop."

But that wasn't what he really wanted, I discovered when a little later we were in the room where Big Sam was reading and listening to the radio news. "Mr. Alberson, do you care if we look at your camp register to see if there've been any visitors from where we come from?"

Big Sam didn't care, so pretty soon Poetry and I were standing at the registration desk, poring over the names of people who had stopped at the camp. I still didn't have any idea what was on his mind, but I noticed he had Circus's note in one hand and was comparing the handwriting of different registrants with the writing that had been in the whiskey bottle.

"What you trying to find?" I asked in a subdued whisper.

His answer was in an indifferent tone. "Needle in a haystack—looks like anyway. You ever see such a guest book?"

I never had. It was the kind of book anybody might expect, though, by the helter-skelter look of things around the place: Big Sam's necktie hanging sloppily and his hair needing combing. Papers and magazines scattered here and there.

The guest book was the loose-leaf kind with a ring binder, and some of the pages were upside down.

A few seconds later Poetry let out a gasp

and exclaimed, "See! Here it is! The same handwriting!"

I looked at the place his finger was indicating, and there wasn't any question at all about the two being the same. The handwriting on the note from the bottle was like that of the name on the register.

"Connie Mae Spruce," I said and thought what a pretty name it was.

"Find anything?" Sam Alberson's deep voice asked in our direction from the chair where he was reading the paper.

"Nobody from Sugar Creek," Poetry's duck-like voice answered, "unless maybe she didn't write her address—and it doesn't give the date."

Sam's voice droned a kind of sleepy reply as he said, "I keep last year's guests on the upside-down pages. That way I don't get mixed up."

Big Sam stood and followed his mustache over to where we were. He looked at the register and at the name Poetry pointed out and said, "That's the woman I was telling you about. She came in a taxi from Lincoln and didn't seem to want to give her address—that's why there isn't any. I should have insisted on it, though, because she left a briefcase in her cabin, and I could never send it to her."

Big Sam turned the guest book upside down, then right side up again, as if he himself was a little puzzled as to which was right, up or down. The phone rang then, and he went to answer it.

Poetry and I bought a bottle of pop apiece,

not wanting the rest of the gang to know what we'd been up to. We worked our way around behind the tent, slipped in, and pretty soon were in our sleeping bags—and also wide awake.

"Why," I whispered to him, "don't you explain what's on your mind—why you wanted the name and address?"

His answer was: "Because I think the woman who left the note in the bottle could be the same one who got drunk in the Wild Horse Tavern at Aspen. When we get there, we'll compare the handwriting we found in the bottle with the register at the Snow-slide Motel, and I bet they'll be the same and the name'll be the same, too. Then we'll know she was here a year ago."

"But that won't solve any mystery," I protested. "We won't know where she is now—not if she disappeared in a blizzard last New Year's Eve."

Poetry's whisper back through the dark was half yawn as he said, "We'll solve that mystery when we get to it."

4

Poetry, Circus, Little Jim, and I were in the tent, Little Jim's parents in one of the camp cabins, and Big Jim and Dragonfly in the station wagon.

For maybe twenty minutes my mind tossed around, trying to go to sleep, wrestling with the different memories I had of what had happened during the day. Once it seemed I was out in the river about a dozen rods from where our tent was pitched, wading along, testing the bottom with my feet, listening to the sound of the riffle singing downstream. I was hearing a chorus of small frogs trilling and every now and then the "gru-u-u-u-umph" of a grandfather bullfrog and the sighing of the wind in the evergreens that grew on the lawn near the motel office.

Then I seemed to be reading a very pretty handwriting that said, "Alcohol is ruining my life. Someday it will kill me. It will do the same for you if you take it into your life."

Also tumbling about in my groggy mind were the last few words of Little Jim's father's prayer, which he had made in the light of the campfire: "Bless all the boys of the world. May those who are happy-go-lucky today not be hardened tomorrow."

I wasn't quite sure what the prayer meant, but it seemed he was asking the One who had made all the boys there are in the world to keep them from getting hard hearts when they grew up to be men.

But it was morning before you could say Jack Robinson, it seemed, and right away we were all up and having a noisy time, breaking camp.

Pretty soon breakfast was over, we were packed, and all of us were in the station wagon except Circus, who was still back in the cabin near the river.

"He's looking to see if we left anything," Little Jim's mother said from where she sat in the front seat beside her husband. "Isn't it a musical day?" she asked nobody in particular and sighed. "Everything is singing—the birds, the water in the riffles, the sunrise. Listen!"

I looked toward the northeast where the red round sun was just nosing its way up over the rim of the horizon. I listened to see if I could hear what *she* was hearing, but I couldn't. I noticed, though, that the prairie all around our wooded camping place was lazy with the smell of sweet clover—and I did hear the singing of tires on the many cars that were already on the highway, racing like mad to get from somewhere to somewhere else.

When Circus kept on not coming, I volunteered to go after him, and before anybody could say no, I was out the car door and on the run toward the cabin.

When I reached the cabin's back door,

which faced the river, I stopped stock-still. *What on earth,* I thought. Instead of Circus being busy looking around in the different rooms, checking to see what, if anything, anybody had left, he was sitting at the kitchen table with an empty whiskey bottle in front of him, writing something on a sheet of paper.

He jumped when he saw me standing just outside the screen door.

"We're ready to go" was all I could think of to say, still wondering what on earth he was doing and why. One reason I didn't say anything else right then was because there were tears in his eyes.

I just stood, staring, asking questions with my own eyes, noticing his jaw muscles tensing and relaxing, tensing and relaxing, the way they nearly always do when he is thinking hard about something.

"I wasn't going to tell anybody," he said, "but I don't care if you know. Here, read it." He pushed open the screen door and handed me the sheet of paper he'd been writing on.

And this is what I read:

If whoever finds this bottle would like to know how to become a real Christian, just write to me and I'll write right back and tell you. My father used to be an alcoholic, and my mother cried most of the time because we didn't have enough to eat, and we couldn't go to church because we didn't have good clothes. Then one day my father got sick of sin and let the Savior have his heart. We have a happy family now.

That's when I got tears in my own eyes—
and it seemed there were some in my voice too
when I gulped and said, "You've got a wonderful *mother* too. I heard my mother say so."

Circus signed his name to the note, put our
Aspen, Colorado, address on it, folded the
paper, pushed it into the quart whiskey bottle,
stuffed the cork in good and tight, and said,
"All right, let's go."

He was out of his chair and pushing open
the screen door and off on a fast lope toward
the river. A way from the water's edge he
stopped, and I expected him to swing back his
strong, long right arm and throw the bottle
with the sermon in it out into the musical
stream. Instead he hurried over to the pile of
drift where he'd found the bottle yesterday,
tucked it in the very same place it had been,
and tied the neck with a piece of string to an
overhanging willow.

On our way back to the car where the gang
was yelling for us to hurry up, he panted, "I've
wasted too many empty bottles. From now on,
every one I find or throw away or leave anywhere is going to have a sermon in it."

Then that sober-faced, brown-haired acrobat astonished me and made me proud of him by
saying, "I might be a gospel minister someday."

I didn't realize I still had tears in my eyes
until I almost ran head-on into a rosebush on
the motel lawn. There was a sad feeling in my
heart but also a glad one. It seemed our acro-
batic, cartwheel-turning, hand-springing, flip-

flopping expert was maybe one of the best boys in the whole world.

Pretty soon we were in the station wagon driving out onto the highway.

All of a sudden Dragonfly, who had just sneezed, looked at me and said, "You got hay fever?"

"No, why?" I asked him.

He sneezed twice before answering, saying, "You're sniffling a little, and your eyes are red."

I didn't bother to answer him, but as our car went singing down the highway, all of us having our usual boys' fun, chatter, and friendly fights, with my mind's eye I was seeing a whiskey bottle lying in a pile of drift, its neck tied by a string to an overhanging willow, and in the bottle a note by one of the neatest curly-headed boys there ever would be. Would anybody ever find the note, I wondered, and write to Circus?

I stayed in my mind's world until Poetry jarred me out of it with a secret punch in the ribs with his elbow. "Look!" he whispered.

I looked and saw in his hand a magazine I knew not a one of us had brought with us. "Where'd you get a *ski* magazine?" I whispered to him.

His answer switched my mind back onto our mystery. "Mr. Alberson gave it to me. Connie Mae Spruce left it in the wastebasket along with several other sports magazines. Because we were going to Aspen, where there is a lot of winter skiing, he thought we might like it."

"Know what?" I asked.

And he answered, "No, what?"

"I'll bet when we get to Aspen, we'll find out she really *is* the disappeared woman."

Our secret was getting almost too big for two boys to carry, but Poetry insisted we still keep it to ourselves for awhile, anyway. There'd be time enough when we found out that the handwriting and the name on the register at the Snow-slide were the same as on the upside-down loose leaf in the Lazywild register.

The farther we went, the faster I felt myself being whirled along into the heart of a strange experience. I just *knew* that when we got to the place we were going to spend our vacation, we'd –we'd–well, you just wait and see, as I had to.

The morning passed, and the afternoon, and we were still headed west. It wasn't until we were driving through the gateway of another camping place to spend another night, that I noticed a corner of the ski magazine had been torn off. Maybe it had been off all the time, but I just hadn't noticed it. I made gestures to Poetry, pointing to the torn place.

He stopped me with a scowl and whispered in my left ear, "It had a *man's* name and address on it. I've got it in my wallet with the note from the bottle. See?"

He showed me the corner torn from the magazine. The name was Charlie Paxton, and the address was Aspen, Colorado!

Now I was like a hound on a trail that was getting hotter and hotter. We certainly had a lot of information bottled up in our minds.

The second the station wagon door was open, Dragonfly swung out, looked all around, straightened his Stetson, and with both hands near his hips where his toy six-shooters were—his high-heeled boots shining in the western sun—he set his face in the direction of a red, statuelike rock and began walking slowly toward it, glaring at it as if it was a cattle rustler or gun-slinger.

All of us must have been thinking the same thing, because we humored Dragonfly by keeping still.

Then, all of a sudden, he growled a surly command to the red statue, saying, "Draw, you horse thief! Draw!"

But the long red rock stood silent. Dragonfly's mind's eye must have seen some imaginary movement of the man-sized rock, because, like lightning, his six-shooters were out, and he was yelling, *"Bang! Bang! Bang!"*

The sentinel rock stood still unmoving and also unshot.

The rest of us piled out and started making camp, as soon as the camp manager told us where we could pitch our tent. Dragonfly wasn't too much help. He was strutting around in his Western outfit as though he was the king of the cowboys, giving commands, using Western language, barking orders in all the cowboy words he knew. His big, broad Stetson certainly looked large on his small head, I thought, and his boots with their high heels weren't any good for running or hiking but would be all right for riding and for showoff. Also, as anybody knows, or ought to know, they could protect him from cactus and snakes.

I didn't have any idea, as we pitched our tent and did a lot of other things Little Jim's dad ordered us to do, that Dragonfly's fancy Stetson was going to play an important part in helping us solve the mystery of the lost woman—or that it would get us into a very dangerous situation.

If I *had* known it, I'd have had a lot more respect for the hat and wouldn't have been so envious of that spindle-legged, allergic-nosed little guy because his folks had let *him* have a high-priced cowboy outfit and mine hadn't let *me*.

Anyway, there I went, *zip zip zip*, into the most exciting part of our Western vacation. Tomorrow we'd be in the Rockies, and in only another half day we'd have our tent pitched somewhere along Roaring Fork River or else a little farther from the town along the shore of Maroon Creek.

Little Jim's mother and Little Jim and the rest of us would attend the Music Festival in the huge tent in the meadow. Then we'd get to see an honest-to-goodness rodeo with Cranberry Jones, my favorite cowboy hero, roping calves, wrestling steers, riding bucking Brahman bulls and— well, it was going to be a wonderful vacation.

Also, Poetry and I were going to spend part of the time doing detective work. We already had some very important clues. Very important.

5

If you've never seen and heard a real, live out-West rodeo, you've missed half the life of a lot of cowboys and of other people who like what is called one of the most exciting spectacles in the world—steer wrestling, trick riding exhibitions, calf roping, and dangerous rides on wild broncs and bucking Brahman bulls!

One reason we were so excited about going to the rodeo was because the advertising placards all over town and the full-page ads in the *Avalanche* almost screamed at us that *Cranberry Jones* was going to perform!

There was a parade in the morning, right through downtown, with beautiful horses and trained dogs and—but I'd better get going right now on what happened that afternoon when I was wearing Dragonfly's hat at the rodeo.

"Just be careful not to let the wind blow it off," he ordered me. "This'll pay you back for letting me wear your jeans and shirt that time mine got all wet in Sugar Creek." And that reminded me of the time you maybe already know about if you've read *Locked in the Attic*.

Little Jim's folks had what are called "box seats," and the rest of us sat on the arena fence, which was a board-and-rail fence with a flat board at the top for people to sit on.

Dragonfly was sitting on my left and Circus on my right. Big Jim and Little Jim were on the other side of Circus, and Poetry was to the left on the end of our line.

It was a wonderful feeling, sitting on an arena fence waiting for the rodeo to start, waiting also for what would be the biggest thrill of all, Cranberry Jones, the cowboy hero who, nearly every time I rode my imaginary palomino back at Sugar Creek, I imagined I was—except when I was the Lone Ranger, who rode a big *white* stallion and wore a mask.

And I guess I had never breathed such clean, fresh air as the kind that swept down from the roundabout mountains.

First on the program was the bareback riding. Two or three different cowboys came out of the chutes one at a time on bucking broncs, stayed on a few seconds, and got tossed off. It was exciting to watch, but I kept waiting and waiting for Cranberry Jones.

All of a sudden, the announcer's voice boomed over the loudspeaker: "Ladies and gentlemen! Cranberry Jones is coming out on brain-bashing, bone-breaking Sudden Death! Sudden Death has been ridden only three times and has unloaded the best cowboys in the nation—killing one and sending the other two to the hospital!"

I sat tense and waiting, chills running up and down my spine.

In a flurry of excited noise up at the farther end of the arena, all of a sudden Cranberry

Jones on Sudden Death's bare back came shooting out of one of the chutes. The horse was charging and bucking as if he was insane.

Cranberry Jones wore spurs on his high-heeled boots. I noticed he was digging them into Sudden Death's shoulder, which was one of the rules for bareback, bronc-busting rides.

That horse should have been named Sudden Death or Sooner! He jumped and twisted and reared and circled and bucked. He exploded all over the place. His four feet flew so fast it looked as if he had ten times as many legs as he did have. He thundered around in every direction there is, including up.

I was so excited with what was happening, hardly able to follow the cyclonelike actions of Sudden Death that I forgot whose beautiful, tan Stetson I had on—*off*, rather, for it was in my hand now, and I was waving it and yelling with everybody else and screaming to Cranberry Jones to hang on.

All the time, Dragonfly beside me was yelling, "Be careful! Be careful! That's my hat!"

But I wasn't careful, not realizing till afterward that he was yelling at me. Also, right that second, I was about to lose my balance and was fighting to keep myself from falling off the fence and landing inside the arena in the path of the thundering feet of that mad-as-a-hornet horse.

Right then is when the canyon wind, which had been having a lot of fun of its own all afternoon, came to life with a fierce gust. It swept across the arena, whipping dust into my face and eyes, and I couldn't see a thing. That, also, is when I really did lose my balance.

To save myself from falling, I let go of the hat. The wind took it and sailed it like a flying saucer out across the arena, where it made a half-dozen topsy-turvy, roundabout, up-and-down movements and landed in the dust in the path of Sudden Death's flying feet!

Just then two furious riders on terribly fast other horses, riders who in rodeos are called "pickups," came charging in behind Sudden Death. Sooner than you could have said Jack Robinson's first name, one of them swept Cranberry Jones off his plunging horse and let him down safely to the ground on his own cowboy-booted feet and—would you believe it?—also on Dragonfly's once beautiful, now-smashed, dusty hat!

Poor Dragonfly's poor hat! Its crown was crumpled. Its swept brim was twisted. It was covered with ground-in dust and dirt!

And then I got one of the most thrilling surprises of my life. Cranberry Jones, instead of hurrying back toward the announcer's stand, turned, picked up Dragonfly's hat, dusted it off, straightened it with a few quick movements, limped over to where we were, looked up at the gang sitting like six chickens on a farm fence, and handed the hat to me—to me because I had reached out for it.

"Things like this happen," Cranberry Jones said "I'll pay for getting it cleaned and blocked. Drop around to the Snow-slide Motel after the rodeo and bring the hat with you." He turned to leave, then looked back and winked at somebody in the direction of the box seats.

"Give it to me!" Dragonfly exclaimed and had the hat out of my hands in a flash. But there weren't any tears in his eyes, and he wasn't angry. Instead, his eyes were shining as if he was very proud to have let his fancy Stetson be trampled by a famous cowboy and by Sudden Death's feet.

Next on the program was the steer wrestling. A half-dozen cowboys I'd never heard of came charging out of the chutes one at a time, riding wildly around the arena in pursuit of a wild-eyed, long-horned steer, swinging off their horses onto the steer's back and wrestling with it, holding it by the horns, trying to pin the steer to the ground, which some of the riders did.

Then the announcer called out over the loud speaker, "Cranberry Jones again, ladies and gentlemen!"

Out came a savage-looking steer with long, pointed, swept-back horns like the handlebars of my bicycle back home. At almost the same time, a beautiful palomino came out, a horse that in the West is sometimes called "the golden one." It was gold-colored and proud-looking with a white mane and tail. On the horse was Cranberry Jones, wearing a coal black hat and a purple shirt with perpendicular gold stripes, and his beautiful high-heeled boots. Behind him on a sorrel horse came another rider.

"The guy on the other horse is a hazer,"

Poetry explained. "He's a cowboy helper"—which I didn't want to hear on account of I already knew it and was just getting ready to tell *him*. Fast and furious, both men chased the long-horned steer! *Gallopety-lickety-swishety-jumpety!* In a few seconds, Cranberry Jones was beside the racing steer and leaning over. In a flash he was half off the palomino and half onto the steer, grasping him by his long horns.

That was one fierce, fast wrestling match between a thousand pounds of hairy, powerful-muscled beef and a hundred-fifty-pound cowboy whose own muscles must have been as strong as the ones on the brawny arms of the village blacksmith, which smithy used to stand under the spreading chestnut tree in our fourth reader in Sugar Creek School.

I took a fleeting few seconds to look toward the announcer's stand, where I knew several men with stopwatches were timing Cranberry to see how long it would take him to throw the steer.

Strain and grunt and twist and snort, flying dust and yelling people—and then, all in a dusty flash, the steer was down! Somebody waved a flag, the crowd broke into wild yells, as did we all. Cranberry Jones had wrestled and thrown his steer in three seconds, less time than he had ever done it before.

After that came the calf roping, and last of all was to be the Brahman bull riding. Well, that fierce old Brahman that came storming out of the chute with Cranberry on his back was faster and angrier than the savage red bull that had gotten into the fight with my cousin Wally's dog, Alexander the Coppersmith, in the story *The Bull Fighter*.

The bull Cranberry Jones was riding had a hump like a camel's hump, except that it wasn't in the center of its back but was forward, near its shoulders. The snorting beast was wilder than the wild horse he had been on.

It took that Brahman bull only a jiffy and a half to throw Cranberry right over his head. My favorite cowboy hero went flying through the air with the greatest of ease and in a few split seconds landed in a dusty, tangled-up sprawl about ten feet in front of the bull's lowered head.

With his head still down, the Brahman stood still for a few seconds, then started on a horns-first dash straight for Cranberry, who by this time was on his feet but staggering groggily around as if he didn't know where he was.

The crowd broke loose with yells, screaming for him to get out of the way or it'd really be sudden death. In my mind's eye I was seeing what might happen any second. I was cringing and yelling and also praying, although I don't remember what I said. But I was asking the One who had made the mountains to save Cranberry Jones's life.

Just then, two rodeo clowns, who had been waiting for something like this to happen, rushed in to distract the bull's attention. The snorting beast stopped, stood still again, staring, then whirled off after one of the clowns—and Cranberry was saved. With two clowns horsing around in front of him, the bull got mixed up in his mind, and that part of the rodeo was over.

Little Jim's parents had arranged for us all to go to an afternoon's concert at three o'clock in the big tent in the meadow—that, as you know, was one reason we'd come West in the first place. But I could hardly wait till five o'clock, when we were to go to the Snow-slide Motel to see Cranberry Jones—and for another special reason that only Poetry and I knew.

I won't take time now to tell you all about the first concert except to let you know what happened to Little Jim while we were listening to a thirteen-year-old Czechoslovakian girl tear the piano apart and put it together again, using all eighty-eight keys to do it. The best boy pianist in all Sugar Creek territory got a far-away expression in his eyes as though he was seeing a future with stars in it, and he whispered to me, "Maybe I'll have to miss some of the gang meetings after we get back home. I might be too busy."

"Doing what?" Dragonfly, who was on the other side of him, asked in a whisper, while the thirteen-year-old girl was still thundering up and down the keys like Sudden Death in a rodeo arena.

Little Jim's explanation startled me and also made me proud of him when he answered, "If I'm going to learn to master the piano like that by the time *I'm* thirteen, I'll have to get down to brass tacks. I can't spend so much time just playing."

"Down to black and white *keys*, you mean," Dragonfly answered.

And Little Jim said, "*Sh!* Keep still!" I could see his lips were pressed together tightly and his small jaw was set, as with eyes glued to the stage he listened for all he was worth.

As the girl played, I looked over the heads of hundreds of people to the place where our station wagon was parked. I noticed somebody had fastened onto the front bumper a large green and black sign that said:

RIDE THE ASPEN CHAIRLIFT,
THE WORLD'S LONGEST

One of the first things Little Jim had done when we got to Aspen was to buy out of his allowance a book called *Flowers of Mountain and Plain.* He had already found six different kinds of wild flowers in the meadow and marked the place in the book where it described them. One of the prettiest was the blue columbine. Even while he sat beside me with tense mind and shining eyes, his book was opened to the very first color plate, and I was looking down at the graceful blue and white blossom that is the state flower of Colorado. I thought how much it was shaped like the daffodils that grew along the orchard fence south of the cherry tree back on our farm.

The Czechoslovakian girl was still galloping up and down the keyboard of the Steinway piano, but for a few seconds I was back at Sugar

Creek. I was thinking about my grayish-brown-haired mom and wishing she could come out here sometime and stay a few weeks without having to work a single day. I might not get to spend so much time playing with the gang myself when I got back, I thought. I could maybe get a job and earn enough to help Dad pay for a vacation for both of them.

Poetry was more interested in minerals than flowers. He had already collected a dozen different kinds to take back for his collection, which he kept in a special place in their basement room with his butterflies.

Big Jim, who might be a banker someday, had noticed how many For Sale signs there were on old houses and even on motels. He wondered how much money a man could make buying a house in the winter and selling it in the summer, when there were a lot of tourists—or else buying it in the summer and selling it in the winter when there were hundreds and hundreds of skiers here from all over the world who, next year, might like a place to live without having to pay so much rent.

Circus was enjoying the music. He had a good singing voice and had been taking lessons back at Sugar Creek from Little Jim's mother.

After the concert, I heard Circus sigh as if he had an ache of some kind in his heart. I remembered the secret he had told me back at Lazywild Camp and guessed what he might be thinking. Later, when we passed an old weatherbeaten, abandoned church with broken-down front steps and tall grass, weeds, and wild flowers growing all over the lawn, he sighed again. I didn't ask him anything, but I knew what was in his mind—and in his hurt heart.

Dragonfly still seemed interested in cowboys and guns. He kept his hands close to his hips all the time, ready at a minute's notice to fire an imaginary bullet into some rustler or horse thief or to capture a stagecoach robber singlehanded.

"Where are the stagecoaches?" he wanted to know when we came out of the tent and all of us worked our way through the scattering crowd to our station wagon.

"Goofy!" Poetry answered him. "That was in the *Old* West. This is the *new* West. They shoot each other with music nowadays."

All Poetry got for his bright remark was a scowl. I'd *started* to say, "A scowl and a sneeze," but all of a sudden I remembered that Dragonfly had stopped sneezing and wheezing almost as soon as we got to the high altitude and the breezes came over the mountains.

"Can we go on the chairlift this afternoon?" Little Jim asked his father, and we couldn't. Not until tomorrow morning, when we'd have plenty of time to ride all the way up to the top of Ajax Mountain. We'd plan it so we could get there about noon, and we'd have lunch up there at the place called Sundeck.

It was already almost five o'clock and time for us to meet Cranberry Jones at the Snowslide Motel.

6

Riding toward town in the station wagon, we drove slowly down a back road and past an aspen grove Little Jim's mother wanted to see.

All of a sudden Little Jim let out a yell. "Wait! Stop! Look at all those white butterflies! Hundreds and hundreds of 'em!"

He had yelled "Stop!" so excitedly that his mother, who was driving, slammed on the brakes. The car stopped so fast that I slid off the backseat onto the floor.

"What on *earth!*" Little Jim's father exclaimed at his son. His mother exclaimed the same thing at the same time. It was a duet without any music in it.

Little Jim ignored their disgust at him and pointed toward the small aspen grove, exclaiming, "Right over there! See 'em! Hundreds and hundreds of white butterflies!"

We looked, but all I could see was about eighty-seven one-inch-in-diameter creamy-white mariposa lilies.

"Those aren't butterflies!" Dragonfly disagreed disgustedly.

Little Jim giggled then and said, "Anybody who knows anything about mariposa lilies knows that the Spanish name *mariposa* means *butterfly.*" He settled down then, his eyes on his flower guide, took a pencil from his shirt pocket and marked down the date.

In the breeze, the mariposa lilies did look like hundreds of white butterflies fluttering above the grass and the other shorter-stemmed flowers.

In a little while we were stopping in the parking lot at the Snow-slide Motel and in another little while were behind it, where there was a large outdoor swimming pool the very shape of a mariposa lily. At one end was a sign that said THE WORLD FAMOUS MARIPOSA POOL.

There was a grassy border all around the pool and, every few yards, outdoor lounging furniture and tables with chairs around them.

Right then, from a bathhouse at the other end of the pool, came a bronze, muscular man in a swimming outfit, and it was Cranberry Jones himself.

"Look!" Dragonfly exclaimed. "There he is! There's the horse thief!"

He swung into action. His six-shooters were out, and he was running and shouting, *"Bang! Bang! Bang!"* in the direction of the king of the cowboys.

"Goofy!" Poetry cried and struck out after the spindle-legged rascal. He grappled with him to stop him from making a big fool out of a little one, and they both went down in a tangled-up scramble in the grass not more than four feet from the pool.

It could have been quite a wrestling match—

and *would* have been if the pool hadn't been so close and if Cranberry Jones hadn't been so quick on his feet. In a flash he was after them, and in another flash he had the two young steers pinned to the ground, one with each hand.

He had saved the boys from the pool, all right, but not Dragonfly's hat. There it was now, six or ten feet out in the water, upside down and floating.

In a split second Cranberry Jones was in after it. "This the hat I trampled at the rodeo?" he asked as he shook out the water and brought it to Dragonfly.

You might have thought Dragonfly would have been angry, but he wasn't. He reached for the out-of-shape, soaking-wet hat, and said proudly, "Thanks, thanks a million!"

"Just wait till I get toweled and dressed, and we'll take your hat over to the cleaners—have to hurry before they close," Cranberry Jones said. Then he plunged into the water again, swimming with a very fast crawl stroke toward the other end of the pool and the bathhouse where his clothes were. I thought as he sped along that he was as good at wrestling the waves he was making as he was a stubborn steer in a rodeo arena.

Just then a hostess in a Western outfit came up to Little Jim's father and said, "We start serving in thirty minutes. Your table is over there by the Hello Tree."

I looked in the direction her hand had gestured, and there were three tables under three different kinds of trees.

"The tree whose leaves are waving hello," the smiling hostess explained. "My brother calls the trembling aspen the Hello Tree. Here, let me show you." She led the way along the footpath that bordered the pool to a table near a white aspen.

"Notice the leaf stems," she said. "They're soft and flexible and flat, not at all like most leaf stems, which are stiff. These are like little narrow ribbons. When there is a breeze, the leaves quake, or tremble, like tiny heart-shaped green flags waving hello. You can also hear them talking. Listen!"

We listened, and the sound in the breeze was like a boy crumpling a newspaper.

"The Indians call the trembling aspen 'noisy leaf,'" she said.

It took Cranberry Jones only a few minutes to towel and dress in his cowboy outfit, and soon he was ready to take Dragonfly's hat to leave it for cleaning and blocking. "We'll ride over on Pal," he said to Dragonfly.

Soon we were watching him swing Dragonfly up on his beautiful palomino, swing himself up behind him, and lope away toward town.

"What a brother!" the hostess said and stood looking after the palomino with Dragonfly and her brother, Cranberry Jones, on it.

Well, it was still fifteen minutes before they would start serving, and we had to wait for Dragonfly to come back before we could even order.

It certainly was an interesting place, so Western and different from any we had seen before.

Poetry and I watched our chance, and a little later we were alone near the bathhouse. He whispered to me, "Let's wade in and all the way across, exploring the bottom with our feet. We might find a gunnysack with a woman in it."

It was a ridiculous idea, of course, but it was his way of letting me know what was still on his mind. The water in the pool was so clear you could see the bottom everywhere.

"Follow me," he whispered, which I did, and in a jiffy we were in the reception room of the Snow-slide Motel.

As he had done when we were at Lazywild back in the middle of the United States, Poetry asked the desk clerk politely, "Do you mind if we look through your register? Maybe you've had a few guests from our hometown."

There was such an innocent expression on Poetry's face, and such a polite smile in his ducklike voice, that the extra pretty lady clerk answered, "There just might be. What is your hometown?"

When Poetry told her, she came to life, saying, "Then you're the boys who are Cran's dinner guests tonight!"

In a minute Poetry and I were glancing through the pages of the guest book, looking for a very beautiful, very familiar handwriting —familiar because we had studied the note from the bottle maybe a dozen times since we'd left Lazywild.

The lady desk clerk was busy watering plants in a small greenhouse just off the office so she didn't hear Poetry's whistle or his excited whisper when he said, "Here it is. I knew it'd be here."

I looked where his finger was pointing. Sure enough, the handwriting was the same and also the name—the name that had been on the register at Lazywild—"Connie Mae Spruce."

"And here's the date," Poetry whispered, and there was mystery in his voice. "That's the same week the blonde woman walked out of the Wild Horse Tavern, staggered down the street through a blinding blizzard, and was never heard from again—and her body was never found."

There was a commotion at the office entrance then, and it was the gang looking for us to come out and get our orders taken for dinner. It wasn't until later that Poetry and I got a chance to talk about our mystery and to wonder to each other what to do about it. We'd have to decide sooner or later whether to tell the rest of the gang what we knew.

Just as we left the office, Poetry whispered to me, "I'll bet if we can find that Charlie Paxton, whose name was on the ski magazine, we'll *really* know something."

Dinner under the Hello Tree, with Cranberry Jones at the table with us, was different from any experience I had ever had. He and Little Jim's pop did a lot of visiting about different things. One of the most important pieces of news I managed to hear, but which I already knew, was that the Snow-slide Motel belonged to Cranberry Jones and his sister Lindy, the very friendly hostess who had told us aspen leaves were like heart-shaped hands waving a friendly welcome to everyone.

All the time, though, it seemed there was a sad expression on Cranberry's face as he and Mr. Foote talked about the Old West, how different it was from the new, and how in the old days the way to get rid of wickedness in the country was to shoot or hang all the wicked men.

"Are things different today because men don't hate as much as they used to?" Little Jim's mother asked. "Or is it because people in the new West don't do such wicked things?"

Again I saw a shadow pass across Cranberry's face, and it was then I noticed for the first time the little L-shaped scar on the right side of his chin and wondered what had caused it.

"No, I'd say men don't steal so many horses nor rustle so many cattle, but they still break hearts and kill by degrees," he said and sighed.

The way he said what he said made it seem he was talking about somebody he knew—and didn't like.

After dinner we strolled around town in twos and threes. In a little while we would drive out to our camp on Roaring Fork River and turn in for a good night's rest before taking the chairlift in the morning to the top of Ajax

Mountain—"the longest chairlift in the whole world," Dragonfly kept reminding us.

Poetry and I did a little secret talking about our special mystery when for a few minutes we were alone and looking in the display window of an art shop. I wasn't interested in the different kinds of pottery except that I kept seeing things through my mother's eyes. If she were here, she would have a hard time to keep from going in and buying something for our house and for the other Sugar Creek women to talk about and want if *they* saw it.

Poetry exploded me out of my back-home world by an easy punch in my ribs with his elbow, saying, "There comes somebody out of Wild Horse Tavern! Uh-oh! He's staggering like he's had one too many."

Remembering what I'd heard Dad say quite a few times, I answered Poetry. "If he's had *one* drink, he's had one too many."

Even from as far away as we were, I could see the man's Western shirt had what Mom would call caballero cuffs, and on its front was a design that looked like a desert cactus.

From the art shop we strolled down a side street toward the roller-skating rink, where the rest of the gang would be waiting. It was like walking through a town full of music. Piano, violin, brass instruments, and voices were chasing different tones up and down the scale. Everywhere, all kinds of other instruments were going like a house afire. It was music students, maybe, practicing their lessons or for tomorrow's concerts.

"Look!" Poetry said. "There's a cleaning place. I'll bet that's where Dragonfly's hat is." The sign in the window said Western Hats, a Specialty. A bright light was on in the back, and somebody was busy working. The only light in the front was a small one over the cash register.

Seeing the lone bulb above the cash register, Poetry remarked, "People in the new West will steal, too, or they wouldn't put a light there."

We didn't spend much time at the skating rink—just took a half-hour's fast round-and-round skate before going out to our camp on the Roaring Fork, where we built a friendly fire because the mountain night was cool and we wanted to be comfortable for our story time.

We were all wide awake, talking about the exciting things at the rodeo and what fun we'd have tomorrow on the world's longest chairlift, when I heard the sound of a galloping horse. I quick looked toward the lane that led into our camping place, and it was Cranberry Jones on his golden palomino!

The first thing I noticed besides the golden horse with its white tail and mane was that, instead of his black hat, the king of the cowboys was wearing a tan Stetson that was too small in the crown to fit well.

He swung out of the saddle and handed the hat to Dragonfly, saying, "I thought maybe you'd want it first thing in the morning. You are going on the chairlift, aren't you?"

Dragonfly accepted the hat, set it on his head at an "I'm tough" angle, and stepped into the firelight, his hands at his hips. He had a set jaw and a surly expression on his thin face as he looked up toward the king of the cowboys. "Draw, mister!" he demanded.

Cranberry Jones's eyes had a twinkle in them in the firelight. He laughed, then said to the grim-faced Dragonfly and to the rest of us, "That's for the *Old* West, boys. Nowadays—" He stopped, his eyes searching our faces. Then I noticed he was looking at Little Jim's father and at the Bible in his hands. *"That,"* he said, "is what people need. Wicked men don't need to be shot *so* much as they need to be *changed."*

It was the same thing I'd heard him say back at the Snow-slide but was so different from what I might have expected an honest-to-goodness cowboy to say that I felt a lump in my throat. All of us must have felt the same way, because not one of us said a word for maybe a long time.

Circus was the first to say anything. He said, "My father got changed once by the gospel. He was an alcoholic before that."

Again I saw the shadow on Cranberry Jones's face.

Because Little Jim's folks asked him to, Cranberry stayed for our good-night devotions. Just before prayer time, Little Jim's father asked if there were any special requests, and that's when Poetry and I, who were sitting side by side on a log facing the fire, felt our hands squeezing each other's and I got cold chills running up and down my spine, because Cranberry Jones's request for prayer went something like this:

"Pray for me," he said, "that God will take the hatred out of my heart for a certain man. It's not right to feel the way I do, but up to now I can't help it."

7

For a few seconds there wasn't a word spoken by anybody, and the only sounds were the crackling of the fire as its long flames leaped up like hounds around a coon tree, the soughing of the breezes in the pines, and the music of the Roaring Fork behind us.

Little Jim's mother spoke then, saying to the serious-faced cowboy sitting across the fire from her, "Would you like to tell us about it?"

Cranberry Jones sighed. His bronze face was very sober in the firelight, as if there was a heavy load of some kind on his heart. When he answered Little Jim's mother's question, he didn't say at all what I expected him to. His voice trembled a little, and his words made Circus clench his fists and set his jaw.

Here is what he said: "When I saw you all so happy under the Hello Tree and noticed how, before you ate, you bowed your heads, it carried me back to my old home in Michigan and the cranberry farm where I got my nickname. My father and mother used to do that. I guess you all have read in the papers lately how Lindy and I've given our lives over to let the Lord run them. I'd been a pretty ornery critter for a long time, but I reckon the Savior just kept on riding sign on me till He tracked me down. Now that He's got His brand on me, it's sort of up to me not to be a stray anymore."

Cranberry Jones cleared his throat, swallowed, and a few seconds later he changed the subject. "I reckon God knows what's on my mind, and all you have to do is just ask Him to take the hate out of me."

When he stopped again, I knew that *whatever* was on his mind was going to stay there and that my curiosity wasn't going to be satisfied.

After devotions, Cranberry Jones thanked us all and invited us to come to the Snow-slide as his dinner guests again tomorrow evening. "Lindy and I can do with a little more Christian fellowship, I reckon. You boys like to try an Old West chuck-wagon dinner?"

Different ones of us said we would, Poetry saying it first.

"Enjoy yourselves on the chairlift tomorrow," Cranberry Jones said, just as he started to move out of our fire-lighted circle to where his palomino was tethered to a pine branch. He looked up toward a white moon the shape of the crescent on the throat of a back-home meadowlark and said, "I reckon that's the biggest stadium in the world up there. As Lindy says, your eyes'll be taking a lot of pictures your minds can look at the rest of your lives."

He swung his right arm wide as though he was trying to lasso something high in the sky— something a boy's eyes couldn't see but his heart could feel; something more important, maybe, than anything else in the whole world.

"Let me walk out to the road with you," Little Jim's father said then.

Little Jim himself was quick on his feet to go with them but got stopped by his mother. "They might want to talk a little," she explained.

Also, it was our bedtime, and we had to get into our pajamas and sleeping bags. Poetry and I got to sleep in the back of the station wagon. The rest of the gang would be just outside the tent in which Little Jim's parents were going to sleep. Tomorrow night two others of the gang would get the station wagon.

It was maybe fifteen minutes before I heard galloping hooves going down the road and saw Little Jim's father coming back.

Poetry, beside me on our air mattress, peeked out the station wagon's back window and said, "He walks like he's worried about something."

"Yeah," I whispered back. "I wish I could have heard what they talked about," not knowing that a few minutes later I was going to hear Cranberry Jones's whole sad story as Little Jim's folks talked it over in the tent.

This is how come I got to.

In spite of the fact that I had a lot of things on my mind, just lying on the extra soft air mattress, covered over with a warm blanket, made me sleepy, so when a little later Poetry wakened me with an idea, I was half mad.

"*Sh!*" I said to him.

But he wouldn't be shushed. "I'm thirsty," he whispered back.

"Oh no, you don't!" I answered and covered my ears with my pillow. There went fleeting through my mind the tangled-up story of the watermelon mystery and all the excitement Poetry had gotten into by being thirsty in the middle of the night.

A second later he was sitting up. "Let's go get a bottle of pop," he whispered.

"We'll wake everybody up," I protested.

But there wasn't any use to protest, not when anybody as stubborn as Poetry wanted you to do something. So, as sleepy as I was and as foolish as I thought what we were going to do was, I let myself be coaxed out of my nice warm bed into a stealthy late-at-night sneak through the shadows to the Cola cooler behind the tent. I certainly didn't expect to stumble over a root and fall and land not more than inches from the tent wall, with my left ear even closer—just close enough to hear Mrs. Foote say to her husband, "The poor boy! It's enough to make him lose his mind—having her disappear like that."

I didn't have time to wonder who could lose his mind over who disappeared, because Little Jim's pop answered, saying, "A tragedy like that happening to a new Christian could make him bitter . . ."

I won't take the space to tell you everything I heard while lying on the pine-needle-covered ground in my night clothes between the Cola cooler and the tent, but here in as few words as I can write it for you is most of the sad, mysterious, exciting story:

Last December when Cranberry Jones was down in Arizona performing in a rodeo, he met and spent a lot of time with a lady sportswriter named Connie Mae Spruce. Connie Mae wanted to write a story to be called "Cranberry Jones at Home," so he sent her up to the Snow-slide to meet his sister, Lindy, and to wait till he finished his next performance at Tucson. Then he would fly home, and they'd spend the week after New Year's together.

While Connie Mae was here waiting, she decided to write a special story of the Ski Festival. To *know* what she was writing about, she began to take ski lessons.

"That's where the trouble began," Little Jim's pop's gruff voice said to his wife. "Her ski instructor—the man who is the engineer at the base station this summer—was a social drinker and kept trying to get Connie Mae, who was an alcoholic, to drink with him. And on New Year's Eve he succeeded. She drank all evening at the Wild Horse Tavern, left there about midnight for her room at the Snow-slide, got lost in the storm—and just disappeared."

Everything was so quiet in the tent for a few seconds that I could hear myself breathing. I didn't dare move, because I didn't want them to know I was six inches away, listening. Poetry himself was as quiet as a sleeping possum beside me.

Then Little Jim's mother said back to her husband, "And Cranberry loved Connie Mae and was trying to win her to Christ—that's why he sent her to Lindy—and you think maybe he would have married her if she'd gotten over her alcoholism?"

"That's what he just told me," Little Jim's father said.

Little Jim's mother sighed heavily, and again she said, "The poor boy!"

Little Jim's pop's story to Little Jim's mom there in the dark tent ended something like this: "The thing has built up in Jones's mind to a terrible hatred for the man who gave her that fatal drink. Last week, Cranberry got a license to carry a gun because there's been a mountain lion snooping around the corral where he keeps Pal—and *that* could be dangerous. I'm terribly afraid of what would happen if the two ever meet alone and get into a quarrel."

That was as much as I managed to hear. I'd been lying so long beside the tent wall that when I tried to change my cramped position a little so my arm wouldn't go to sleep, my foot accidentally struck the tent rope and shook the whole tent.

"What was *that?*" Little Jim's mother's worried voice exclaimed. "Maybe the mountain lion's hanging around our camp!"

I crouched there, cringing, waiting for them to start talking again, so I could sneak away. It seemed I had heard things they might not have wanted me to but which Poetry and I almost *had* to know to solve the jigsaw puzzle mystery we were working on.

A little later, when we were back in the station wagon, Poetry whispered, "Do you know what?"

"No, what?" I asked.

"I'm still thirsty. We forgot what we went after."

Well, I told Poetry everything I had heard, he told me everything *he* had heard, and we talked until we were sleepy again. Something was really worrying me. *Cranberry Jones has hate in his heart for somebody. Cranberry Jones has a special permit to carry a gun.*

But the next thing I knew it was morning on the Roaring Fork. The gang was making a lot of boy noise. There was the smell of breakfast cooking on the camp stove, and in a little while it'd be time to hurry over to the base station and begin having the time of our lives riding the world's longest chairlift.

8

Riding the world's longest chairlift was a little disappointing at first. It wasn't half as exciting as riding a roller coaster, and there wasn't anybody yelling and screaming with excitement.

But it *was* kind of scary as the chair I was riding alone in swung out over the tops of the trees. I could tell I was a *little* frightened when I noticed I was holding onto the bar in front of me so tightly my knuckles were white. Maybe it was partly because every now and then the wind would change into a strong gust that would sway my chair and blow the hair on my hatless head into my eyes. It was a sunshiny day, though.

In my left hand was an illustrated folder with information about the different ski runs, but it wasn't easy to read with the wind ruffling the pages and the treetops below swaying dizzily.

About sixty feet ahead of me, in a chair all by himself, was Little Jim. From behind he looked like a small brown mouse. Even as far away as I was, I could tell he was looking down, studying the terrain below, maybe trying to see if he was riding high over any new kinds of wildflowers.

The higher my chair went on its steeply sloping cable, the more wind there was, since there wasn't anything up here to break it. I kept wondering how Dragonfly was getting along.

He had decided to wear his swept-brim Stetson —"to keep the sun out of my eyes," he had explained. I turned around to look and, after watching only a few seconds, could see he was scared half to death. He was all hunched up, holding onto the bar in front of him with one hand and onto his hat with the other.

I yelled back down to him, "Why didn't you leave your hat in the station wagon like I said?"

But he didn't answer, not even a word. He just held on.

Behind *him*, in his own chair, was Big Jim and behind him Circus and last of all Poetry. Little Jim's folks had taken the first two chairs and were way up ahead of their small son.

There was another cable to my left, and on it were other people in chairs coming down. Every few minutes one would pass me.

And for a few minutes I was in the history section of my imagination, remembering the Bible story of Jacob's ladder, the dream a boy once had when he was asleep in a very rocky place with only a stone for a pillow. In the dream, the boy saw a long ladder—or maybe it was a stairway—reaching all the way up to heaven. And there were angels going up and down on it.

It was easy for my mind's eye to imagine the members of the Sugar Creek Gang, with Little Jim's parents leading us, on our way up to heaven. Except that not one of us looked like an angel, and I happened to know that most of the time not a one of us acted like one.

I was exploded off my dream ladder right

then by a wild yell behind me. Dragonfly's high-pitched tremulous voice sounded like a hound breaking out in full cry on a hot coon trail. I quick turned, and what to my wondering eyes should appear but something flying through the air to the left of our chairlift, sailing high like a giant bird toward the Little Nell T-Bar slope, where beginners learn to ski.

Whatever it was, it zoomed into the sky, darting wildly, dropping a few dozen feet, then whirling up and away again. I needn't have wondered what it was, though, because below me in his swaying chair was a spindle-legged little guy with his hair in his eyes, and there wasn't any hat on his head.

Dragonfly's Stetson had been whipped off by a fierce, fast gust of wind and already was far away, flying along a lot faster and with a lot more ease than a man on a flying trapeze. I was too far away to see the little guy's expression, but I could feel the worried wind that must have been blowing in his mind. I quick yelled to him, "Let it go! You can't stop it, anyway! We'll go get it when we come back down!"

Nothing important happened the rest of the way up. There wasn't anybody to talk to—only to yell at, and that would have been unfair to the people riding down on the chairlift.

As I kept on riding and looking at the scenery, I had my mind on Dragonfly's hat sailing out into the wild blue yonder, wondering where it would land and would we ever find it.

I was also studying the folder in my hand.

Maybe sometime when I got older I could come to Aspen in the winter and go swishing down the different runs: The Dipsy Doodle, Ruthie's Run, The Silver Queen, and all the others.

At a place called Midway, which was the upper end of the lower lift, we all got off one at a time and changed to the chairs on the upper lift, the way people in the city change buses. Then away we went, on and on, up and up, till we got to Sundeck Cafe at the very top. There we swung out of our chairs to relax awhile before taking the long ride back down to the base station.

Little Jim had brought along his flower guide. While we were having our lunch in the 11,300-foot-high restaurant with other people eating all around us, he had it open and was studying it.

Dragonfly was still worried about his lost hat, and the rest of us were a lot more quiet than we would have been swimming and diving in Sugar Creek.

After lunch, we took a sightseeing hike up the ridge, higher and still higher, and I realized my eyes were writing things and taking colored pictures I could look at the rest of my life whenever I was in my mind's special world.

When we were halfway back to Sundeck, all of a sudden Dragonfly exclaimed, "Hey! Where's Circus?"

I looked back up the ridge we had just hiked down and saw a boy's blue shirt sleeve. The rest of the boy was behind a twisted, dead juniper trunk. "I'll go back and get him," I volunteered and started.

I found Circus sitting on a rock, looking out over the thousands of acres of fir and pine and spruce and millions of wildflowers of many varieties.

He must have been concentrating on something far away, because he didn't hear me until I was only a few yards from him. Or maybe the wind up there was blowing the sound I was making *down* the hill rather than toward him.

Anyway, I heard him before he saw me, for the wind was blowing his words down into my ears. I didn't get any whole sentence, but he wasn't talking to me anyway. I guess maybe he hadn't intended any human being to hear him. What he said was a Bible verse I knew: *"The devil took Him to a very high mountain and showed Him all the kingdoms of the world and their glory; and he said to Him, 'All these things I will give You, if You fall down and worship me.'"*

I was hardly breathing, because I didn't want to interrupt whatever Circus was thinking about.

He finally heard me, though. He quick stood up, looked at me maybe thirty feet down below him, and called, "Be there in a minute!"

He had a faraway expression in his eyes as we walked down the ridge together, and I knew his mind was back up where he had been.

One thing he said before we got down to the Sundeck, where the gang was waiting, made me feel fine inside: "Bill, maybe I'd never have been a Christian at all if you hadn't started me going to Sunday school a long time ago. Remember?"

I remembered. If you want to, you can read all about it in the book called *The Swamp Robber,* which is the very first story there ever was about the Gang.

Well, we still had the long ride ahead of us before we could go over to Little Nell Beginner's Slope and the Wild Horse Canyon area to look for a flyaway hat. That was where it looked as if maybe it had landed after its high ride on the wind.

It was Dragonfly who found the clue—stumbled over it, that is—and fell sprawling. He started a small avalanche with himself in the middle of it. When he came to a stop twenty feet or more from where he had started, he was lying in a tangled-up scramble, with the shoulder strap of a woman's leather handbag caught on the toe of his right cowboy boot.

He also was lying upside down on my stomach, which felt like it had a ton of weight on it instead of only eighty-seven pounds of spindle-legged boy.

The small avalanche of rocks and dirt went tumbling on down the canyon we all had been exploring, looking for the lost hat.

For a brain-whirling second, I forgot we were looking for a tan Stetson that had blown off a boy's head two hours before. When I saw that weather-stained, scratched-up, woman's hand-tooled handbag with the mariposa lilies carved on it, I wriggled myself from under

Dragonfly, caught hold of the shoulder strap, rolled to a sitting position, held onto a root to keep from sliding farther downhill and let out a yell to all of us. *"Look, gang! Look what I've found!"*

It took us all only a few minutes to get together to see what I had found, which Dragonfly said *he* had found because he had stumbled over it and it had accidentally caught on the toe of his boot.

"Let's see what's in it!" Big Jim said, reaching for it.

"Maybe it'll have a hundred dollars in it," Dragonfly said excitedly. "If it does have, it'll be mine because I found it. 'Finders keepers, losers weepers.' And I'll get the reward too!"

"Finders are *not* keepers when it's something like this." Big Jim corrected Dragonfly's quote. "You turn things like this over to the police and let *them* decide what to do with it."

Just hearing the word "police" made me realize we had something serious on our hands.

Big Jim, who now had the leather handbag in his own hands and was holding it out of reach of any of the rest of us, had another idea. "It maybe belongs to some woman who lost it when she was taking a hike—a tourist who's staying right now in some hotel in the area."

"Or maybe somebody attending the Music Festival," Little Jim piped up to say.

Circus, who had been quiet all this time, his jaw muscles working, his clear, dark eyes studying the scratches on the handbag, spoke up then and startled us by saying, "Those scratches were not made by accident. Those are *tooth* marks. Some wild animal has been gnawing on it!"

I was surprised then to hear Dragonfly say, "The same wild animal that ate up the disappeared woman! That's how come nobody ever found her!"

It was such a startling idea that for a second it seemed Dragonfly's imagination had given us part of the answer to the mystery. It'd be easy, I thought, for Connie Spruce, who had been drunk and had started home from the Wild Horse Tavern at midnight in a blinding blizzard, to wander off into the mountains, stumble along through the drifts, and a mountain lion or a pack of wolves find her.

I hadn't any sooner thought that, than I said it.

We all acted pretty tense while our minds were imagining that kind of terrible story.

Well, we couldn't just sit there on the side of a canyon in a little huddle around a tooth-marked handbag, which was also covered with dirt stains and was pretty badly weathered. We couldn't just keep on saying everything and doing nothing.

So Big Jim, being the leader of the gang, unfastened the handbag's leather strap and lifted the flap-over top. All our eyes were quick inside, looking at all the woman's stuff that was there. Honest, if a boy carried that many different kinds of junk in his six or seven pockets, his mother would wonder, *What on earth!*

9

What a surprise. There we were in Wild Horse Canyon, a woman's just-found, tooth-marked handbag in front of us, and in the billfold Big Jim had in his hand was a picture in full color of Cranberry Jones, one of the best-known cowboys in the whole country. My thoughts were as snarled as a boy's fishing line after he's just lost a fish and both pole and line are caught in a thicket of willows.

"Hey!" Dragonfly burst out. "There she is! I'll bet that's her picture, herself!"

His topsy-turvy way of saying what he'd just said didn't seem to matter right then, because right in front of my eyes in another of the billfold's windows was a full-color snapshot of a girl wearing a Western outfit, smiling. She also was on a horse. *And the horse was a proud looking golden palomino with a creamy-white mane and tail!*

"Here's an ID card!" Big Jim announced, and in a second my astonished eyes were seeing in another plastic window the words "Approved Identification Card."

Poetry's squawky explanation in my ear then was *"And look! It's Connie Mae Spruce! The name is Connie Mae Spruce!"*

Now we'd seen the name *three* times. Poetry and I had, anyway—once on the camp register at Lazywild, again on the register at the Snow-slide, and now on an identification card in a weather-stained, tooth-marked leather handbag!

Also, we'd *heard* the name last night while we were just outside the tent in our camp on the Roaring Fork!

Poetry whispered in my ear something else then, saying, "The handwriting is the same!"

And it was.

Double what on earth! This was the fourth time we'd seen the very pretty handwriting: Once on the Lazywild register, once on the Snow-slide register, now on the identification card, and, maybe most important of all, on the note Circus had found in the whiskey bottle, the very sad note that said, *"Alcohol is ruining my life . . . Someday it will kill me . . ."*

It looked as if the pieces of our jigsaw mystery were going to fit together. The name of the woman who owned the handbag, who had camped at Lazywild and left the note in the empty whiskey bottle, was Connie Mae Spruce. She had attended the Ski Festival last winter, learned to ski on the Little Nell T-Bar Beginner's Slope, liked skiing so well she had dared the more dangerous runs, and then, one day, the morning of December 31, she had gotten a letter from somebody. That letter had made her very sad.

She was *so* sad she had tried to drown her trouble in drink.

All these thoughts flashed into and out of my mind in a split second, it seemed.

I say out of my mind, because right then Big Jim let out a whistle and an exclamation and said, "And here's a letter with Cranberry Jones's name in the upper lefthand corner!"

The postmark on the letter was Tucson, Arizona, and the date was December 28 of last year!

Dragonfly cut in to say, "That's it! That's the letter she got that made her so sad she wanted to be a dead cat at the bottom of the creek, so she tried to drown herself in drink!"

I glanced quick at Little Jim, and his face looked like somebody had stabbed him in the heart.

I guess maybe each of us had a different idea in his mind. Circus, who has a hunter for a father and knows more about wildlife than any other boy in the Sugar Creek territory, had been examining the teeth marks on the handbag. In one place one of the mariposa lilies was almost completely scratched away.

"It was a *porcupine!*" he suddenly burst out. "Porcupines are crazy for salt. They'll chew on shovel handles, belts, saddles, old shoes—anything man's hands have handled. But a porcupine couldn't or wouldn't ever eat a human being."

Dragonfly came out then with what was on *his* mind. "Let's don't forget what we came here for in the first place. Let's get going looking for my lost hat!"

"Wait!" Big Jim's face was pretty grim. "Let's bring it to a vote to decide what to do with the handbag. If it belongs to the woman who disappeared last New Year's Eve, we ought to give it to the police or the sheriff, and we ought to do it maybe right away. We can come back tomorrow for your hat."

"Yeah," Poetry exclaimed to Dragonfly. "Your hat's not so important, anyway."

That got him a surly look from Dragonfly, and there might have been a scuffle there on the steep canyon side, but Circus, who had a good mind, suggested, "Maybe we ought to give it to Cranberry Jones first and let *him* give it to the sheriff or the police. If he wrote her that letter, he'll maybe know who she is—or was."

We quick brought it to a vote, and all of us except Little Jim voted yes to read the already opened letter to see if there was anything in it that would help us decide whether to give the handbag to Cranberry Jones first or to take it as quick as we could to the police.

Little Jim said, "I think we ought to ask my folks what to do. That letter was private, and we don't want to open and read a letter somebody wrote to a woman that's maybe still alive somewhere—and it's none of our business."

So, in spite of our majority vote, Big Jim closed the handbag, fastened its leather strap, and said, "All right then, let's get going."

"What about my *hat*?" Dragonfly piped up. "I'm not leaving here till we find it."

Again Poetry told him, "I say it's not so important. We're on the trail of a mystery that could mean life or death."

But it was important to Dragonfly, so pretty soon, with Big Jim carrying Connie Mae Spruce's handbag, we were working our way around the Little Nell T-Bar Slope and all over what seemed everywhere, looking for a flyaway hat.

It was a little like exploring a giant-sized river bottom to see if it was safe for swimming, except that we were wading through thousands of mountain wild flowers, the names of most of which I didn't know yet but was fast learning. Little Jim every now then let out a squeak and said that he had found a this or that flower.

After about fifteen minutes more of looking, Dragonfly, off to my left and quite a ways below me, let out a war whoop, crying, *"Here it is! I found it! It's as good as new!"* He came grinning and panting to where the rest of us were and bragged, "It's the most important hat in the world, maybe." He had it on at an angle that said he thought that he, himself, was important. Then with his hands near his hips, he set his thin jaw savagely, glared at Poetry, and demanded, "Draw, mister! Nobody can say what you said about my hat and get away with it! Draw!"

But Poetry wouldn't draw—not having anything to draw, anyway. "You can shoot me in the back if you're coward enough to," he said with a grin. He turned his back as a target, and that ended the feud between two good friends.

Dragonfly did shoot Poetry with words, though, and what he said made good sense. "If

80

I hadn't had the hat on when we were on the chairlift, it wouldn't have blown off, and we wouldn't have had to come looking for it, and we wouldn't have found the disappeared woman's handbag—and if there's any money in it, it'll be ours. I say the hat is important!"

Poetry turned like lightning and shot back, "Finders are *not* keepers!"

It wouldn't take us long to get to the Snowslide, where my stomach had been telling me for quite awhile it wished I would hurry up and take it. Little Jim's idea that we ought to give the handbag to his folks first still seemed right, so away we went as fast as we could.

"Looks like it's closer to go past the base station," Big Jim said. "Come on. Step on it, gang." With that, he broke into a run—a kind of short-of-breath run because the altitude around Aspen was about seven thousand feet above sea level and we weren't used to it yet. We soon were all so short of breath we had to slow down to a walk.

Because what we'd found could be very important, we did quite a lot of talking, each of us saying what was on his mind.

Big Jim puffed to us an idea that showed what a good imagination he had. "You guys remember last night at camp devotions, Cranberry Jones asked us to ask God to take the hate out of his heart for somebody? All right then, I've got it figured out that Connie Spruce was a special friend of his. Somebody else wanted her for *his* friend. The two men had a fight, and that's how Cranberry got that new L-shaped scar on his chin."

"What I can't figure out," Poetry panted beside me, "is how did her handbag get back there in Wild Horse Canyon if that's who she is—or *was*—if she's still alive."

"Sure," Dragonfly put in. "Like I said, she got eaten up by a wild animal of some kind."

That's when Poetry reached out his hand and stopped me. Then he stopped the rest of us with his voice, saying, "Wait a minute, everybody! Bill and I've got something to tell you. Something the whole gang'd better know."

I was ready to stop anyway. I had just that minute accidentally stepped on and crushed into the ground the purplish-red blossom of an inch-tall, ball-like, spiny-stemmed flower that Little Jim would want to look up in his book. It was different from any mountain flower I'd seen yet.

"It's a *purple cactus,*" the flower-guide carrying guy said the second he saw it. "I've been looking for one all afternoon."

"When you *should* have been looking for my hat," Dragonfly barked. He had his hands at his hips again, ready to draw.

Poetry started in then, telling the rest of the gang as fast as he could what he and I knew, beginning way back at Lazywild with the note in the whiskey bottle and hurrying on to the present minute where we all were with the handbag in our possession. Then he surprised me with some brand-new ideas I hadn't even thought of myself. "Remember how Dragon-fly's hat blew off in the wind while he was high up on the chairlift?"

"Sure," Little Jim piped up.

"All right," Poetry went on, "if a *hat* could fall from the chairlift, couldn't a woman accidentally drop a handbag while she was up there?"

We were only a couple of hundred yards from the base station now, and I could hear the big motors humming. "I get it," I said, as we all decided to hurry on. "Connie Spruce accidentally, when she was away up there somewhere, dropped her handbag. A porcupine found it and dragged it all the way down to Wild Horse Canyon where *we* found it."

Poetry quickly stooped, picked up a small colorless stone, tucked it into his pocket, saying, "Topaz," then went on with his idea. "No, you *don't* get it. Here's what I mean. If a *hat* could blow off on a windy day, or a woman could accidentally drop her handbag, couldn't the woman herself also lose her balance and fall off if she was riding a chairlift at midnight in a blinding blizzard, especially if she was drunk at the time!"

I quick looked far ahead, up and up and still up, at the long line of sixty-feet-apart chairs on the long cables stretching from the base station toward Midway. The chairs, all empty now, swayed high over treetops and huge boulders and canyons and gullies. I cringed at the idea of anybody's falling off one of the chairs.

But Poetry's idea seemed the best one we'd thought of yet. Maybe we had the mystery almost solved as to what had happened to the disappeared woman.

Even Dragonfly forgot—for a few minutes, anyway—how important his hat was and what a famous Old West marshal his imagination had been telling him *he* was. He came out with a bright idea of his own. "Yeah, and the woman who left the note in the whiskey bottle at Lazy-wild and who left the ski magazine there—the one Poetry told us about—came here to the Ski Festival last winter. She's the one that got drunk at the Wild Horse Tavern and started home in the blizzard. She got lost, stumbled into the base station, got on a chair, and started up. Her chair swung along, climbing higher and higher, and she was so cold she could hardly hold onto the bar in front of her—and didn't know what she was doing, anyway. The wind was blowing so hard, and she just had sense enough to be scared, so she tried to jump out and maybe she did—or maybe she accidentally fell out, and her handbag with her, and landed in a snowdrift as big as a house, and she got buried deeper and deeper and finally went to sleep like people do when they're about to freeze . . ."

Dragonfly was talking along so fast and with such good sense for a change that not a one of us cut in to interrupt him. We let him race on to the end of his idea.

"She finally froze to death and wolves or

84

mountain lions or wildcats found her and ate her. Then in the spring there was an avalanche, and her skeleton with the handbag got carried all the way down to Wild Horse Canyon. And if the sheriff will send out a hunting party and dig all around close to where we found the handbag, they'll find her bones."

Little Jim spoiled most of the story, though, by saying, "But they wouldn't have the chairlift going at midnight in a blinding blizzard!"

Right then, Big Jim took a quick glance at his wristwatch and ordered, "Come on, gang! We'll be late for supper if we don't hurry!"

10

I quick looked at my watch and was surprised to discover how late it was. We were supposed to be at the Snow-slide in only a few minutes, and we were still quite a ways from there!

"How about letting me carry the handbag the rest of the way?" I asked Big Jim.

"It's my turn," Dragonfly coaxed in a whiny voice, adding as a reason, "It was my hat that had sense enough to blow off and land in Wild Horse Canyon, and it was my new cowboy boot's toe that caught on it. I want to walk right up to Cranberry Jones and hand it to him myself."

And that is how it happened we got to read Cranberry's letter to Connie Mae Spruce.

We were all swinging along, walking pretty fast toward the base station, which was on the way to the Snow-slide, when I heard a yell from Dragonfly. I looked quick in his direction and saw him sprawled on the ground, with the handbag and almost everything in it scattered all around him. That is, everything was scattered around him except the letter, which was in his right hand. That little rascal had opened the handbag, taken out the letter, and was sneak-reading it as he walked along. Not seeing where he was going, he had stumbled over an old aspen log and fallen head over heels.

Big Jim was pretty grim when he swooped down upon Dragonfly, pried the letter out of his clutching hands, and scolded him. "We decided *not* to open it! You've gone against the whole gang!"

Dragonfly pouted up at him, while different ones of the rest of us picked up the things that had fallen out of the handbag and put them back. "Little Jim voted against the whole gang! *We'd* voted to read the letter! I was just doing what we *voted* to do!"

Of course, he was right even if he was wrong. Anyway, now that the letter was already open and part of it had been read by part of us, we decided maybe it would be all right if the rest of us read the rest of it. And it was a good thing we did. I'll tell you why in a minute.

When Big Jim read the letter out loud, here is what my astonished ears heard:

Dear Connie,

It was such a thrill to get your letter telling of your good times at the Ski Festival. How I wish I could be there now to take some of the runs with you, but that pleasure must wait till after New Year's, when I will have wound up the roping, riding, and wrestling season down here. I'll be rushing to the nearest plane, Connie, and when I get to Denver, will charter a special to fly me to Aspen. I'll have to leave Pal here, because I do have a couple rodeos in California before spring. Next summer, I'll ship him home. Now that Lindy and I own the Snow-slide, we plan to make it our headquarters, and Pal and I will go into retirement together.

I hope you don't mind my being a little jealous of Charlie. He's a good ski instructor, which may partly account for your learning so well so fast. I hope you don't mind what I'm going to say next, Connie. New Year's in the past at Aspen has been a bit too partyish. With drinking so popular nowadays, you'll find it a lot easier if you'll spend most of the time with Lindy. Charlie is quite a drinker. Now that you've gone so many months without a drink—well, you know how much a certain cowboy down in Tucson cares. Enough said there.

One thing more, though. Charlie does have times of depression when he acts very strange. He's a spoiled boy, and when he doesn't get his way, he can be very difficult. I am very sorry to learn from Lindy that he has proposed marriage, for—well, I must tell you—he already has a wife and two children down here. I met her yesterday. One of the first things she asked when she saw me was, "Does Charlie still have his spells of despondency?"

While Big Jim was reading aloud to us, I had the feeling that we were hearing what wasn't supposed to be our business. But when he read the next paragraph, I was glad he did. Part of it was:

To really retire, Connie, a cowboy needs a wife. You may consider this a proposal if you like. But if you don't like a proposal by letter, I'll ask you in person when I get there. I wouldn't hurry it up like this, but I want you to know that I believe in you, that I believe you'll never drink again. We'll let the past be forever past.

The rest of the letter *wasn't* any of our business, and since it isn't any of yours, either, I won't write it for you. We quick put it back into the envelope.

Big Jim closed the handbag and was going to carry it himself the rest of the way to the Snow-slide, but when Dragonfly begged so hard and promised so tearfully he would be careful, Big Jim let him. That's how it happened that when, a few minutes later, we reached the parking area of the base station, that spindle-legged little guy had Connie Mae Spruce's handbag hanging by its strap on his shoulder.

The chairlift motors had stopped, and all the chairs on both cables up and down the long slope were swinging empty, which meant everybody was already down and the lift was closed for the day.

We swung past the base station building, and my heart was beating fast as I wondered if the engineer was *really* Charlie Paxton, and if he was . . . well, if he was, what then?

"Everybody wait a minute," Poetry said. "There's something I want to ask the engineer."

"Not *now!*" Big Jim ordered him, adding, "We've got to hurry on!"

"Now," Poetry said grimly and quick puffed to the open door of the engineer's room.

I followed him in, seeing first of all a big sign on a bulletin board that read DO NOT TALK TO THE ENGINEER!

And then I saw the engineer himself. Of course, I'd seen him before, but this time I really noticed him. And what to my wondering eyes should appear but first of all his Western shirt with caballero cuffs and on its front a design that looked like the purple cactus I'd stepped on a half hour ago back on the mesa. Also he was limping a little.

Poetry smiled his famous smile and asked, "Sir, may we ignore that order?"

"We're about to wind things up for the day." The engineer had a gruff voice and a mustache the size of an eyebrow. He looked at all of us a little impatiently. "I guess you can ask *one* question." He seemed a little bored.

Poetry's question was, "Could *anybody* who happened to push that lever right there start the chairlift?"

The engineer eyed Poetry's innocent face with a question mark in his dark eyes. "Anybody could," he said indifferently. He turned his back, sat down at a black-topped desk, opened a register of some kind, and started to study it.

Poetry was not satisfied with just one question. He popped another. It was startling even to me, but I wasn't prepared for the way it exploded the man into action. Poetry's all-of-a-sudden question was, "Did you come down here in the middle of the night of December the thirty-first last winter in a blinding blizzard and find the motors running and the chairlift going—and turn it off?"

The man in the Western shirt with the purple cactus design on its front spun around in his swivel chair and barked, "Listen, sonny, there's a sign up there! And I *am* busy!" He opened a drawer at his right, took out some kind of record book, and shoved the drawer closed, but not before I had seen what looked like a revolver. In that fleeting glimpse, I noticed the gun had a blue barrel and a walnut grip.

But it wasn't what I saw in the desk drawer that seemed so important to the man with the mustache. Instead, it was what *he* saw when Dragonfly, who had been just outside the door, came bursting in to say, "Hurry up, you guys! I'm hungry! I'm—"

The engineer's eyes focused on the handbag hanging by its strap on Dragonfly's shoulder. He sprang out of his swivel chair, staring and exclaiming, "Where did you get *that*?"

Right that second I heard outside the sound of galloping hooves and saw through the window somebody on a beautiful palomino headed straight for the base station where we were. It was the king of the cowboys in his black Stetson and black shirt with the gold stripes, coming maybe to find out why we were so late for our chuck-wagon dinner.

The muscular engineer must have seen and heard, also. He made a dive for Dragonfly and demanded, "Here, sonny, let me have that!"

And that's when something clicked in my mind, the way an alarm clock sometimes clicks a fraction of a second before it goes off, and I knew, *knew,* that the base engineer was for sure the man whose name had been on the ski magazine—and also that Charlie Paxton was the man Cranberry Jones hated but didn't want to and couldn't help it!

I let out a warning cry to Dragonfly. "Don't let him have it! Run! Run for your life!"

And Dragonfly ran. That rascal of a spindle-legged, scared little boy, still believing maybe that finders are keepers, streaked toward the door.

Charlie Paxton also streaked toward it and got there first. Dragonfly ducked out of his grasp, swung past me and around behind the office desk with the panting engineer right after him.

There was plenty going on in that office, I tell you—and in a few minutes there'd be still more when Cranberry Jones came in, which he was bound to do to see what was going on and why.

Dragonfly was like a mouse in a house with a woman with a broom after him. He dodged this way and that and that way and this, then toward the door of a room just off the office. But he didn't make it. Charlie got there at the same time and in a flash had him in his clutches. That is, he had one arm.

And that's when our basketball practice back home came in handy. Dragonfly made a quick, over-his-head pass in my direction. The handbag came flying through the air with the greatest of ease. I made a leap for it, caught it, and came down in Charlie's arms.

The alarm clock in my mind went off again, and this time it was my temper catching fire. I wasn't going to let Connie Mae Spruce's handbag get into the possession of the man who had maybe been to blame for whatever had happened to her. I ducked, squirmed, twisted, and with a *wham-wham-wham* with my spare fist on the man's stomach and chest and chin, I broke loose. I started on a headfirst dash for the open door and ran *ker-smack* into Cranberry Jones, who had heard such a commotion he had sprung from his horse to see what was in motion.

Now *what* do you do at a time like that? When you are in the middle of dangerous excitement like the one we were in. You have a lost-and-found handbag belonging to a lost-and-not-yet-found woman. In the handbag is a picture of Cranberry Jones on his palomino. And you are absolutely sure the woman whose picture is also in the handbag has been frozen to death and eaten by wild animals after her fall from a chairlift. What *do* you do at a time like that?

I had been running so fast when I whammed into Cranberry that I bowled him over, and the two of us went down in the graveled parking area five feet from the still-open base station office door.

It took us several seconds to get untangled.

And that's when Cranberry saw the handbag—although I could tell by the startled expression on his face that it wasn't the *first* time. I held it out to him, saying, "We found it this afternoon away over in Wild Horse Canyon."

For a second there was a scared expression on his face as he stood staring at the handbag. His jaw was set, and I could feel how hot his temper was and what a hurt heart he had.

Circus shattered the tense silence right then by saying, "Those teeth marks were made by a *porcupine*. Porcupines don't eat people."

I think I realized he was trying to say something cheerful, trying to make Cranberry think Connie Mae Spruce was still alive. But it seemed he only made him feel worse. "No," the cowboy said, "porcupines don't. But mountain lions do."

And *that* made me think of the mountain lion that had been sneaking around Pal's corral and of the pistol Cranberry Jones right that minute probably had in a shoulder holster. Also, it reminded me that there was another revolver in a desk drawer just behind the engineer.

11

Even though there wasn't a gun in sight, there were bullets in Cranberry Jones's eyes and another expression in Charlie Paxton's—if the engineer *was* Charlie Paxton. It was a sort of wild expression as if he was half out of his mind. The way they were glaring at each other, their jaws set, was like two dogs back at Sugar Creek, standing looking at each other and growling and waiting for one or the other to make a move. Then with a flurry of flashing tempers and slashing teeth, the dogs are headfirst into a barking, snapping, growling, yelping fang fight.

I certainly never expected things to take the turn they did right then, for I never dreamed what was going on in Little Jim's mind. But I might have guessed it, knowing what a kind heart he had, and how, back at Sugar Creek when he'd been looking through his tears at his drowned kitten, he'd sobbed, "Father, forgive them, for they do not know what they are doing." Also, every now and then, when it seemed the right time, he'd quote a Bible verse, one of the more than a hundred he knew by heart.

Anyway, right in the center of the whirlwind of anger and hot temper and hate I could feel all around us, that friendly little fellow called out in his cute little mouselike voice, "Everyone who hates his brother is a murderer!"

Just that second there was the sound of an engine at the farther end of the parking lot. I saw it was Little Jim's father and mother in the station wagon, also having come to look for us, wondering maybe why six ordinarily hungry boys were late for a chuck-wagon dinner we'd been looking forward to all day.

It was like having to stop fishing when the biting is extra good, to have to leave and go to dinner. Harder than that was to understand why, all of a sudden, there didn't seem to be any fight in Cranberry Jones's mind. "All right, Charlie," he said. "The boys're coming over for a talk about *this* later!"

Even though his tone of voice was like a kind hand stroking a kitten, I could feel that Charlie, the kitten, didn't like it and any second might get mad and start scratching, which our old Mixy cat does when you stroke her fur the wrong way. When Cranberry said "this," he'd held up the handbag by its shoulder strap. And when his eyes met Charlie's again, there was fire in them.

The word "Charlie" struck my mind kind of hard. Now I *really* knew that the base station engineer was Charlie Paxton, whose name had been on the corner of the ski magazine and who had asked Connie Mae Spruce to marry him when he already had a wife and two children.

This, for sure, was the man Cranberry Jones

hated and didn't want to. Before long there'd have to be a showdown between the two.

Little Jim's folks, not knowing what a whirlwind we were in, called out to us, "Hurry up, boys! It's way past six o'clock!"

And we hurried—all except Cranberry, who took a little extra time to get to his palomino, taking Connie Mae Spruce's handbag with him.

All the time while we were having our chuckwagon dinner in a grassy enclosure behind the Snow-slide and just across from the mariposa swimming pool, I kept thinking about our mystery, worrying about what had happened to Connie Mae Spruce and what Charlie Paxton knew about what had *really* become of her. I didn't get to fully enjoy the very different kind of dinner we were having. Our big tin plates were heaped with all kinds of cowboy chuck taken from the back end of the wagon, and we were eating outdoors at a redwood table. You can't worry and enjoy eating at the same time.

I wasn't the only one that was worrying, and I didn't have half as much to upset my mind as Cranberry. First, as we always do when we eat in a public place, we waited with bowed heads till each of us had finished thinking his thanks to God.

I should have kept my eyes closed a little longer, I suppose, but for some reason I didn't. Instead, I was studying Cranberry's set face. His eyes were looking straight ahead. I turned to see what he was staring at, and there wasn't a thing there except the six-foot-high stockade fence about fifty feet away

Poetry must have had his eyes open a little early, too, because the minute the silent prayer was finished and everybody was talking to everybody, with nobody listening to anybody, my pumpkin-shaped friend whispered to me, "Remember what he asked us to pray for last night?"

As soon as I could get a word out around the corner of the bite of barbecued beef I had just taken, I answered, "Yes, and the man he hates is Charlie Paxton, and Charlie Paxton is the engineer at the base station!"

Right then Dragonfly raised his voice and demanded, "Why doesn't anybody *listen* to me? I'm trying to tell you how I found a woman's handbag this afternoon—with porcupine teeth marks on it and with a picture of Cranberry Jones in it and another picture of a woman in a riding outfit on his horse, and there was a letter in it to her from Cranberry and—"

Well, because Little Jim's parents hadn't heard the story yet, quite a few of us started in helping Dragonfly tell what we knew, but we got cut in on by Cranberry, who, with an indifferent voice, said to the Foote parents, "So many people write to me for pictures, I had a few thousand made last year, and Lindy sends them out."

What, I thought, *on earth!* And I also thought, *He doesn't know we read the letter he wrote her.*

Poetry answered Cranberry then, saying, "I

wonder how she got a picture of herself riding on your horse."

Cranberry gave Little Jim's folks a knowing look that seemed to say, "We might as well keep as much from the boys as we can." Then he answered Poetry. "There are a lot of palominos around the country. They all look alike. A girl could get quite a charge out of showing the two pictures to her friends."

Imagine that! And imagine anybody thinking what was going on was too exciting for six boys with grown-up minds to know about! Why, right that very second we knew as much about the mystery—and maybe more—than Cranberry himself!

After we'd finished our chuck-wagon dinner and there was a little time left before Little Jim's folks were going to the evening concert in the big tent—the gang was not going but *would* go tomorrow afternoon to the Youth Concert —Poetry and I moseyed around the mariposa pool. We stopped a minute at the Hello Tree, listening to the ribbon-stemmed aspen leaves to see if in the evening breezes they were actually talking. And then just that second, when there was an all-of-a-sudden breeze, I could actually hear voices.

The only thing was that when the breeze had passed, there still were voices, and they were the voices of two men just outside the stockade fence.

"*Sh!*" Poetry whispered. "Listen!"

I didn't need any shushing or his order to

listen. The voices belonged to Cranberry Jones and Little Jim's pop.

Poetry and I quick crouched under the low branches of the aspen and crawled cautiously to the fence, getting there just in time to hear Cranberry say, "I phoned the police about the handbag. It's the first big clue they've had in the case, thanks to the boys. I know Charlie knows a lot more about what happened to her than he'll tell. I'm afraid he got her drinking on New Year's Eve. Did it knowing she was an alcoholic. And *if* he did, that makes him a murderer. And I'm a murderer, too, for hating him —as that fine boy of yours reminded me today. *'Everyone who hates his brother is a murderer.'* Mr. Foote, God'll really have to help me. I'm afraid of what I might do if I meet him alone! He's a scoundrel, a cheat, and an ungodly wretch. When I think of his sweet little wife and two precious children I met down in Arizona—needing a husband and father, without enough food and clothes . . ."

I heard Cranberry Jones sigh heavily.

I had to strain my ears to hear Little Jim's pop answer, for right then Lindy called for Cranberry to come to the phone. I did manage to hear him say as they moved away from the fence Poetry and I were crouching behind, "Did it ever occur to you she might still be alive somewhere?"

I also heard part of Cranberry's answer, which started like this and faded out as they got farther away, "How *could* she be? Nobody could live in a blizzard like that. I'm sure if she were alive she'd want me to know it. She'd write and tell me and . . ."

If only we could have heard more, but we'd heard that much, and it was a good thing we did. It started Poetry's detective-like mind to working again. Suddenly he let out a gasp, grabbed me as if he was a mountain lion trying to kill a horse, and exclaimed, "I've got it! I've got it! Little Jim's pop is right!"

"Got what?" I exclaimed back.

"Connie Mae Spruce is alive! The whiskey bottle we found at Lazywild proves it! Why didn't I think of it before?"

"Whiskey bottle proves what?" I asked, wondering how a whiskey bottle with a note in it, found in a pile of drift along a river back at a tourist camp in the middle of the United States, could prove Connie Spruce, who had fallen from a chairlift in a blizzard and frozen to death—how could it prove she was alive?

But I didn't have as keen a mind on things like that as Poetry, which I can prove by his astonishing answer. "Wasn't that pile of drift at least a year old, washed there from upstream somewhere?"

"Sure," I said, "what of it?"

"What *of* it!" he exclaimed, scoffing at how slow I was to understand. "That whiskey bottle with the note in it was a *new* bottle! The label was still on it, and it wasn't even dirty! It hadn't been washed there from somewhere upstream!

She put it there herself the week before we camped there. She's still alive! I know it!"

"But," I protested, "she camped there a year ago this summer! Her name was on one of the upside-down pages. Remember?"

That seemed to stump Poetry for a second. But he quick had an answer. "That depends on whether that *page* was upside down or whether the *guest book* was."

Right then Little Jim's mother called to us. They were ready to drive us to our camp on Roaring Fork where the gang was going to stay until after the concert.

I was surprised to find everybody already in the station wagon, waiting.

"Where on earth have you been?" Big Jim was a little cross. "Remember our rule about staying together? We don't want any of you little kids getting lost!" That was a friendly insult we knew better than to get angry at, as it would have proved we *were* little in our own minds.

It was going to be fun being all alone in camp, sitting around the fire, telling stories, making plans for the rest of our vacation, talking over all the excitement of the day so far.

I wondered, as we drove past the place where yesterday Little Jim had called out about the white butterflies, whether Poetry would decide to tell the rest of the gang what we thought—what we'd almost decided back under the Hello Tree—*that Connie Mae Spruce was honest-to-goodness-for-sure still alive!*

Pretty soon we were there and alone, had a

good fire going in the safe place the forest service had shown us, not more than a hundred yards from the Roaring Fork and maybe only one hundred feet from an abandoned log cabin an old settler had built there years and years and years ago.

It was one of the finest feelings I'd ever had—lying on my sleeping bag, enjoying the warmth of the fire, which felt good in the cold mountain night air, looking up at the stars and the new moon, dreaming about the family who had lived here long ago, wondering how many children they had had, and how dangerous it had been with wolves and mountain lions in the mountains roundabout.

I was jarred out of my reverie by the sound of an engine on the road leading to our campground. Then a car with four lights turned into the lane and came toward us, its headlamps almost blinding me.

The car's third light was a powerful spot, and its fourth was a flashing red light on top.

"Police!" Circus exclaimed.

I rolled over and up to a sitting position. Not being used to police cars stopping at our house back at Sugar Creek, I felt my muscles tightening, my jaw setting, and my nerves trembling for wondering, *What on earth?*

A few seconds later the car was all the way up to where we were, as close as it would be safe for a gasoline motor to come to an open fire, and a gruff voice called, "You boys all alone here?"

Big Jim answered that we were, and the same voice asked, "Seen anything of a man on a horse?" Now the spotlight was sweeping the whole area, shining toward the river and the abandoned cabin and far back into the round-about trees.

Dragonfly piped up from the other side of the fire, "What's Cranberry Jones done?"

I looked across to him and to my surprise he was standing, his Stetson at a savage angle, his hands near his hips. He was glaring as well as blinking, and his thin little jaw was set fierce-ly as though he was an Old West marshal. Any second now I expected him to explode with a bark, demanding, "Draw, mister! Draw!"

The voice from the car answered Dragon-fly's question, saying, "Just making a routine investigation. Are you the boys who found a handbag this afternoon?"

"I'm the boy," Dragonfly answered proudly. "Some bozo named Charlie tried to make us give it to him. He chased me all around the chairlift office trying to get it away from me, but I passed to Bill and he ran *ker-smack* into Cranberry Jones and bowled him over, and we gave the handbag to him. He's got it now."

What Dragonfly had just said, excited and bragging, didn't seem to interest the police. They raced their engine a few seconds, then the one with the gruff voice said, "Jones'll be riding in after a while. Tell him we have news for him and to wait here till we get back."

The car with the four lights drove away, and

we were alone again to think and to talk over all the excitement. This might be the new West but there certainly was a lot of the Old West in it. I had a creeping feeling that somebody might be watching and listening to us from the old cabin on whose log face the leaping flames were making weird shadows right that minute.

The police hadn't been gone more than a few seconds before there was the snap of a twig behind our tent, and a man's voice whispering to us from the shadows.

"Hey, fellows! It's me, Charlie Paxton! I want to talk with you!"

12

We didn't have time to say yes or no, whether or not we wanted to talk with the base station engineer who had acted so strangely in the afternoon, for there he stood, blinking a little at the brightness of the fire.

Poetry mumbled in my ear, "He's wearing his gun!"

I'd already seen his wide belt with the leather holster hanging from it and, in the holster, the walnut grip of a pistol shining in the firelight.

Behind us was the roaring of the Roaring Fork, and all around and above us the soughing of the wind in the evergreens that circled the clearing where our tent was pitched. But louder than any of the sounds nature was making was the pounding of my heartbeat in my ears. It seemed as I looked at Charlie's grim face, and as my eyes strayed to the log cabin behind him, that maybe he'd been hiding there all the time, listening to everything we'd said to each other. Maybe the police had been looking for *him* too, as well as for Cranberry.

It certainly was a tense minute, as we waited to see or hear or have a part in what was going to happen next—if anything was.

Nothing did happen for a time, not until

we'd talked a little while with Charlie. He seemed nervous and worried and scared.

"You boys may think I acted strange this afternoon, the way I tried to get the handbag away from you. But I'd seen it or one like it before. It looked just like one that belonged to one of my ski students last winter. You want to tell me what was in it? Any identification?"

Dragonfly answered for us. "It had Cranberry Jones's picture in it. On his horse. And a *woman's* picture, on his horse. That's why we gave it to *him* instead of you."

Charlie nodded grimly. "She was registered at his motel. She's the woman you boys maybe know about who disappeared last New Year's Eve in a blizzard. The police all over the country've been looking for her. I thought maybe there might be a clue of some kind in the handbag—some hint as to what might have happened to her."

Charlie raised his head then, listening, and a scared look came over his face. His right hand moved toward his holster.

Right then is when the thump-thump-thump of the heartbeat in my ears changed to the thuddety-thud-thud of a horse's galloping feet. Then I saw a man on horseback swing into the lane and come loping toward the firelit circle where we all were.

I saw the reflected light on the horse's eyes first, then the horse and the rider on it—and it was Cranberry Jones on his beautiful palomino.

Pal hadn't any sooner come to a stop than

Cranberry was off and in full view in the fire-light. Charlie Paxton—whose name had been on the corner of the ski magazine we'd found at Lazywild, and who had tried so hard to get the handbag away from us in the afternoon, who was a scoundrel, a cheat and an ungodly wretch—was now face to face with the cowboy whose voice I'd heard many times in Old West radio programs and whose six-shooter on those programs had shot many a rustler or bank rob-ber. These two men, who I knew were enemies, were going to have a showdown right in the middle of our campfire light!

This, my imagination was screaming to me, was going to be *the real thing!* I, myself, in actual life was going to see an honest-to-goodness-for-sure Old West duel. This wasn't any little old pretend radio or TV story. This was for real!

Both men's faces were set. Both stood stiff-legged, reminding me again of two Sugar Creek dogs standing nose to nose just before flying into a fierce, fast fang fight.

I looked quick to see if Cranberry Jones was wearing his gun, and I couldn't see any, but the way he was holding his right hand close to his chest told me he *had* one in a shoulder holster under his jacket.

I don't know why I thought what I thought right then, but even while we were in the mid-dle of what any second could be a quick-draw duel, I remembered last night. At about this same time, Little Jim's father was asking the One who had made all the people in the world to help more people love other people. It seemed it was going to be hard for God to answer that prayer. Any second now, there might be a flash of fire from a pistol, and one of the grim-faced men would be dead. Or else two guns would spit bullets at the same time, and *two* men would be dead!

Right then Cranberry Jones's voice fired a round of bulletlike words. "I reckon this is the showdown, Charlie. I don't know what has happened to Connie, whether she is alive or not. All I know is that you were seen last New Year's Eve, midnight, leaving the Wild Horse Tavern right after she did. You caught up with her at the church corner. You know, Charlie, and I know, and the town and the whole country knows, she never reached her room at the Snow-slide. I'm asking you once more—what did you do with her?"

Hearing that, I got the feeling that Cranberry Jones was like Mixy, our black and white cat, stalking a field mouse in our south pasture —only this time the field mouse could fight back.

Charlie Paxton's voice had a tremble in it, but his words were pretty fierce. "Don't force me to do something I don't want to, Cran! Stop! Don't come one inch closer!"

I hadn't noticed Cranberry coming nearer until Charlie shouted that. Then I saw that the two men were at least two feet closer to each other than they had been.

Now it was Charlie Paxton who was our old

cat. Cranberry Jones was only another *neighbor* cat, and pretty soon there would be a fierce, fur-flying fang fight.

Jones's answer was: "I said a minute ago, Charlie, *This is the showdown!* The boys' finding Connie's handbag and the way you acted there this afternoon proves you do know more than you've told anybody!"

As the gang waited, tense and cringing, Charlie Paxton began to talk.

"I've told you a dozen times. She broke away from me out there in the snow and ran toward the mountains. I hurried after her, stumbled into the blind alley behind the church, and lost her.

"I fought my way through the storm to the Snow-slide, thinking she might have made it home, but she hadn't. That's when I decided to try the chairlift office. We'd had a lot of talks there that week. It took me almost a half hour to get there, the storm was so terrible.

"When I finally reached the door, it was open, the motors were on and the chairlift going. I couldn't remember turning it off. I'd been drinking a little myself—a little more than usual because of the weather forecast. The blizzard was supposed to last all the next day and maybe longer, so I didn't have to worry about having a clear mind. I—"

Cranberry Jones's savage voice cut in right there, accusingly. "And you gave *her* a drink! You *knew* she was an alcoholic, that she didn't dare touch a drop or she'd be off again on a binge. You *knew* she was trying to quit and hadn't had a drink for months and was winning the battle against the stuff!"

I, Bill Collins, cringing beside Charlie Paxton, could feel the black wrath in Cranberry Jones's voice and the hate-fire burning in his heart.

Charlie looked a little like a caught mouse, I thought. His right hand was still close to his holster as he hurried to finish what he wanted to say.

"I shut off the motors, then I went back to town to look for her. And that's all I knew till the next morning, when I found her purple scarf out by the lift where many a time I'd seen her slide into the chair when it moved past. That's when I knew what had happened—or thought I knew. I'd left the chairlift going, and Connie, not knowing what she was doing, had swung on and gone up into that wild blizzard. When I stopped the motors, she must have been stranded up there somewhere between heaven and earth and had frozen to death!

"I was *afraid* to tell the whole truth. I hoped and hoped all the rest of the winter and spring and up until today that she'd turn up alive somewhere. But now I know there's no use hoping. The handbag proves what happened to her. Tomorrow they'll start searching all over again, and this time they'll find her. *Wait!* Let me finish. You've got to believe me, Cran. I've lived with this all these months, lying awake nights, fighting against the awful fear and guilt at what I'd done. But now I know. I've murdered her just as truly as if I'd taken her life deliberately. I . . ."

All this time Charlie had been standing with his hand close to his side, as if any second he would use on Cranberry Jones the blue lightning he had in his holster. I couldn't tell if he was really sorry for what he was to blame for, or if he was just trying to keep Cranberry from shooting him. It *seemed* he was only scared that what he'd done would cost him his life.

Maybe I was a little more sure than any of the rest of us that he *would* use his gun—or maybe I was the only one who was keeping an eye on the twitching fingers of his right hand. Any second now, I thought, something violent might happen. Charlie was like a lit firecracker with a spitting fuse racing toward the powder.

And then, right in front of my eyes, there was a lightninglike movement toward his holster, and that's when I screamed bloody murder to Cranberry Jones. "Look out! He's going to shoot!"

Talk about things happening fast! At the same second—or maybe even sooner—there was a flash of fire and a deafening explosion.

When what few wits I had gathered themselves together and I was able to think straight in all that whirlwind of excitement, there were three people on the ground only a few yards from our campfire—Charlie Paxton, Cranberry Jones, and Big Jim, our powerful-muscled leader.

I'd had a fleeting glimpse of Big Jim making a flying leap for Charlie's knees like a tackle tackling a quarterback. I'd also seen Cranberry Jones duck, as if trying to dodge a bullet. Both of them were diving toward Paxton just as the blue lightning from Charlie's holster spit fire from its muzzle and that thunderous explosion shattered the silence of the mountain night.

For a few seconds the three on the ground in the firelight lay with their arms and legs all tangled up. Cranberry was on his knees, holding Charlie's pistol wrist with both hands, trying to keep him from shooting again. Charlie was grunting and struggling and exclaiming and trying to get away. Then he began to scream hoarsely, fighting like a wildcat to get his pistol hand free.

Big Jim was holding onto Charlie's legs for dear life, also grunting and with a set face.

It seemed I ought to hurl myself into the middle of all that writhing, grunting, sweating scramble, yet for some reason I stood frozen, scared and all mixed up in my mind.

13

If I had been in there holding onto one of Charlie Paxton's legs, maybe he wouldn't have been able to do what he *did* do right then. He gave his powerful body a heave, kicked Big Jim's grip loose, rolled over and onto his feet, and was free!

I was so close to him I could have reached out and grabbed the pistol in his hand, but remembering one of my dad's favorite expressions, "It's better to have good sense than it is to be brave," I stayed stock-still, scared but trying to use what little good sense I had.

Right then, Circus called out, "Somebody's coming!"

It was the police car again, its red light flashing and its spotlight searching our camping area, lighting up the shrubs, the old cabin, the roundabout trees.

Well, you never saw a man move faster in your life. Charlie Paxton whirled, grabbed me around the waist, jabbed his blue lightning into my back, and growled to me, "Don't make a move or you're a dead boy!" And for some reason it seemed it was the right time to have good sense instead of being brave, which I wasn't anyway.

I felt myself being pulled backward, pulled

and half dragged toward the abandoned cabin.

What was going to happen now? What would my folks say and how would they feel when they read in the papers that their only son had been kidnapped and shot by a wild man? And how would Charlotte Ann, my baby sister, manage to grow up without a big brother to look after her?

Where, also, would I be three minutes after the bullet from Charlie's blue-barreled pistol went sizzling through my heart or head or somewhere—and how much would it hurt?

Even while I was still being pulled backward, what good sense I still had reminded me that the Savior had died for my sins and that I was a saved boy as far as my soul was concerned. If I *did* get killed, I would go straight to heaven.

It was my *body* that needed to be saved from whatever was about to happen to it, if anything was.

Still using me as a shield between him and the fifty-yards-away police, Charlie reached the log cabin, the pistol muzzle still pressed into my ribs. Right then the searchlight found us and pinned us to the cabin wall, and there came a strong, deep voice over a loudspeaker ordering, "All right, Charlie! You haven't got a chance! Throw down your gun!"

Charlie's voice shot back, "You'll never take me alive!"

What he said was yelled past my right ear, and that's when I smelled what at first was like a

Sugar Creek polecat. Then I got another strong whiff, and it was a whiskey smell, which meant that Charlie Paxton, who was acting half scared to death anyway, wouldn't have a clear mind. Now I knew I would *have* to do exactly what I was told.

The spotlight was still on us, and Charlie was still behind me with his whiskey breath, the pistol muzzle was still in my ribs, and I was still not brave.

The loudspeaker shot a different kind of message to Charlie then: "All we want is for you to tell us what you did with Connie Spruce. Let the boy go and tell the truth, and it'll go a lot easier for you!"

That must have made something in Charlie's mind snap. Though he'd been acting like a man scared half to death, now he let loose a wild scream, crying, "I killed her! I got her drunk, and she started the chairlift and got on! I turned it off and left her stranded up there somewhere, and she froze to death!"

There was something about what he said, and especially the way he said it, that made him truly seem a wild man. His powerful left arm around my waist was crushing me to his chest so tight I could hardly breathe. I didn't dare try to fight my way free on account of the pistol muzzle still in my side.

The police didn't dare risk a shot at him either. They might miss him and hit *me*.

"Come on, you!" Charlie snarled in my ear.

I didn't know what he meant by "Come

on," but when I felt myself being forced toward the east end of the log wall, I knew he was going to try to get to the corner and behind the cabin. Once there, he could soon lose himself in the woods. He could cross the Roaring Fork and hide out in the mountains—maybe *never* be captured.

There wasn't a thing I could do except nothing, and I was doing that the best I could and at the point of a gun. If only I could make a quick whirligig movement and sink a fist into the pit of his stomach, then maybe I could knock the wind out of him.

Charlie was mumbling to himself and sobbing now while he inched his way along with me toward the corner. In a few seconds we'd be there. It was what he kept on saying over and over that made me decide for sure he was losing his mind: "I killed her! I killed her with a bottle! I made her drunk, and she went up the chairlift in a blizzard. They'll never get me alive. I'll kill myself first!"

It was as if he didn't realize I was even there, yet I was being almost crushed, his arm muscles were so powerful.

The word "bottle," though, was like a doctor's hypodermic needle with good sense in it being jabbed into me. Charlie Paxton *hadn't* killed Connie Mae Spruce! Connie Mae was still alive somewhere! Her name was on the upside-down page of the upside-down guest book in Lazywild Tourist Camp back in the middle of the United States! If Charlie should commit suicide, it'd be for nothing. Whatever had happened the night of the terrible blizzard, Connie *hadn't* died.

That thought was like a burning fuse in my mind. I had to save Charlie's life. *Had* to. I tried to talk, but my voice was cut off by his powerful left wrist pressed against my throat. "She's not dead! She's alive!" I tried to say but couldn't get out a single understandable word. I could only make squawking noises like a young rooster learning to crow.

Dad's advice about good sense was still in my mind, but how could I have good sense when I didn't have any good sense to have! One thing for sure, I *had* to stop a suicide. I was the only one that could do it!

I gave my body a fierce fast twist and felt Charlie's arm muscles tighten, his wrist press against my throat, choking me. If only I could do what a Sugar Creek coon does when a hound has him at bay and he is fighting for his life . . .

That thought was the first sign of good sense I'd had for a while. Quick as a flash, I twisted my head sideways and sank my teeth into Charlie's forearm, just above the last snap of his caballero cuff.

Charlie let out a yell and relaxed his grip—and that's when I whirled and sank my right fist into the pit of his stomach, driving it with muscles that felt as strong in my mind as the village blacksmith's.

That, I tell you, was one time in my life I

was glad I'd had to do a lot of hard work on the farm and had developed my muscles till they were strong. Charlie not only let out a yell when I bit his forearm, but when my fist exploded in the pit of his stomach three times in rapid-fire succession, he grunted, grimaced, and sank to his knees.

That's when I saw the gleaming barrel of his gun lying in the grass and his trembling hand fumbling for it. Like a streak I was after it. I swooped down upon it, grabbed it up, stumbled and fell, rolled over and onto my feet again, and was off like a freed coon for the campfire where the gang and the police were.

14

I certainly didn't have any trouble seeing my way to the campfire, for I had the police car's headlamps lighting the way. Also, almost the minute I had Charlie's pistol in my hand and had started to run, another car came swinging into the area.

There was plenty of action now—the police racing for Charlie before he could get his breath after I'd knocked the wind out of him, Cranberry Jones hurrying over to the car that had just driven in, the gang talking excitedly about what had happened and was still happening.

By having good sense instead of being brave, I'd not only saved Charlie from killing himself but maybe had saved my own life as well. Who knows what he might have done to me? He was so mixed up in his mind with whiskey and fear and six months of worry about what he thought he was to blame for.

I won't have room enough in this book to tell you some of the other exciting things that happened on our out-West vacation. But maybe you'd like to know that it was Lindy, Cranberry's sister, who drove into our camping area while we were in the middle of all that danger and excitement.

Two women were in the car, Lindy and a golden-haired lady beside her. I happened to be near enough to hear what Cranberry Jones exclaimed when he got there.

"*Connie Mae!* Where did you come from? How did you get here?"

I didn't get to find out why Connie Mae had come—and from where—until the next morning when we were all having breakfast at an outdoor table near the Hello Tree.

"It was the note some thoughtful person left in a whiskey bottle back at Lazywild Camp that made me decide to come." She looked with the prettiest, kindest eyes I ever saw at Circus Brown, who had written the note, put it in the bottle, and fastened it there in the pile of drift. "I'd left my briefcase at the camp with valuable manuscripts in it. I went back to get it. And when I decided to go out to the pile of drift where I'd left a note in the bottle myself, I found *your* message."

Again the blue eyes smiled at Circus, making me proud that he had thought of doing what he had done and had had the kind of heart that made him want to do it in the first place.

The morning breeze shaking the aspen leaves was making them sound like a hundred chattering voices, and the same breeze was making friendly little waves on the surface of the pool, sending one *big* wave of homesickness over me for the sound of red-winged blackbirds in the bayou.

But it was still interesting where we were, because I was hearing one of the most exciting true stories in the world, maybe.

"You boys had left a copy of the *Aspen Avalanche* too," Connie went on, "and I saw the news item about the $500 reward for information leading to my capture—I mean, my *whereabouts*." She smiled across the table at Cranberry Jones's extrahappy face. "So I decided to come back and claim the reward myself! I remembered your letter last winter about plane service, Cran. To get here as soon as I could after arriving at Denver, I chartered a plane, got to Aspen late yesterday afternoon, and came over by taxi but arrived here just too late to help save poor Charlie from taking his own life. But you didn't need me, I see." Now the blue eyes were smiling at *me*, and all of a sudden I was maybe the most important hero in the world.

Lindy spoke then. "We still don't understand how you survived in that terrible blizzard."

"I still don't know, either," Connie Mae said. "But let's say it was the hand of God. I was still in a half stupor when I began to realize where I was—on the chairlift, going up. The weather was so cold that if I hadn't had on my ski outfit, I think I'd have frozen. But I *did* have: woolen socks, sweater, pants, mittens, and even my overmittens and boots—all that plus my coat. And of course, as you all now know, my handbag.

"How I got onto the chair or how the lift happened to be going, I don't know, but I prayed desperately it would keep on going till I could get to Midway. Maybe I could find shelter there and stay till the storm ended, I thought.

"But all at once the cable stopped and of course my chair with it, and I was stranded, high above the mountainside. Even as warmly dressed as I was, the wind was driving through my outfit, and I was shaking with the cold and from being afraid."

There wasn't a one of us at the table that wanted to interrupt.

Connie stopped a few seconds, bit her lip, swallowed, and I saw tears in her eyes, as for a fleeting minute she seemed to be staring at something just above the top of the stockade that surrounded the pool. "You must have been praying, Lindy," was what she said before going on. "I thought maybe it wasn't far to the ground, and if I should jump out, I'd probably land in a drift—if I didn't land in a treetop or on a pinnacle of rock.

"I thought of my flashlight in my handbag and fumbled for it. Because my fingers were all thumbs, I dropped the handbag. I lurched forward to try to stop it, lost my balance and fell, and did land in a drift."

The rest of Connie Mae's story was just as exciting. She knew that every sixty feet on the cable above her there was another hanging chair, and every now and then, all up and down the mountain, there was a tower. She shined her light up through the swirling snow and managed to see the shadow of the chair she'd just left. Maybe she could use the *chairs* for markers. She knew her direction would always be down, never up, but there would be places where the chairs would be too high for her to see even their outline.

"But I *did* make it," she finished, "all the way down to the base station. The door was locked, but I found a window, opened it, crawled in, and the warmth made me so drowsy that I fell asleep on the couch. In the very early morning when I awoke, the storm was over, but I had a terrible hangover. A hangover conscience is very tormenting. What a fool I had made of myself the day and night before! Now that it was morning, what was I to do? I simply couldn't face you, Lindy. I couldn't!

"But thinking of you gave me an idea. So many times in the past, when I'd had a lost weekend, I'd go to the nearest stable, rent a saddle horse and ride. Ride and ride and ride. The wind in my face, the fresh air, and the feeling of flying would help clear my mind.

"So at dawn, I hurried from the base station, through the deserted streets to the Snowslide stables, and saddled Ginger—you know, my favorite—and while the town still slept, I rode away, out past the meadow onto Highway 82, which had been plowed the day before but now was badly drifted.

"Such a beautiful world, I thought. The mountains roundabout, a million snow-laden Christmas trees. Everything was so white except my heart. I wasn't worthy of my friends . . ."

Connie Mae Spruce stopped her story again. There were tears in her eyes. But when she began once more, her voice was calm, the way maybe the Sea of Galilee had been in the Bible after the Savior stood up in the boat and said, "Peace, be still!" to the storm and the white-capped waves.

"That," Connie Mae said, "was before I knew what I know now—that with the power of God, *any* alcoholic who is sick of himself and the sin of drinking that helped to make him an alcoholic and really *wants* to be free, *can* be free . . ."

The rest of Connie's exciting story, if I wrote it all for you, would make this book too long. I'll have to wind up my part of it right now and then let you read what the *Aspen Avalanche* printed about her in their next week's edition.

When we ourselves read it, the gang was home again, our vacation over, and all of us were down by the Snatzerpazooka tree near the swimming hole. We were going swimming for the first time since coming home.

Dragonfly's important Stetson was hanging on the left shoulder of Snatzerpazooka, who was swaying lazily in the Sugar Creek breeze. From across the cornfield there came the musical *"Oucher-la-re-e-e-eeee"* of red-winged blackbirds in the bayou. Dragonfly, who had forgotten how to sneeze while we were in the mountains, had learned in a hurry as soon as we were halfway home—which meant he would have to go back to the mountains next summer and stay till the first fall frost, maybe. And the rest of the gang might get to go along.

And then Big Jim took from inside his shirt a copy of the *Avalanche*. "It came in the morning mail," he said. "You guys want to read about the wedding?"

"What wedding?" different ones of us asked him, and he answered lazily, "Oh, Cranberry Jones and Connie Mae Spruce."

It was a pretty wedding story. Cranberry and Connie were married on the backs of two beautiful palomino horses—Pal and Ginger—beside the chuck wagon at the Snow-slide Motel. Cranberry was going to quit the dangerous business of roping, riding, and wrestling and live a quiet life—stuff like that.

And then at the bottom of the story was an editor's note that said:

Thus ends another "happy ever after" story, solving only in part, however, the mystery of how a woman can disappear in a midnight blizzard and never be heard from again until she wants to be. Mrs. Cranberry Jones's own story of her harrowing escape from a midnight ride on the chairlift and her early morning horseback ride on the beautiful Ginger from the Cranberry Stables ended with another unsolved mystery. Three weeks of her life are missing. For she has no memory of anything that happened after she had ridden only a mile or so out on Highway 82 toward the airport—nothing until she came to herself three weeks later in Lincoln, Nebraska.

One guess is as good as another, but the editor would like to propose that she rode all the way to the airport, and that now, with all the publicity about the case, some plane or helicopter pilot will recall that on the morning of last New Year's Day a woman in a ski outfit chartered a ride from there to Denver.

Old Joe Campbell's heart attack that New Year's morning sealed forever any story he could have told about why Ginger was standing outside the stables, saddled and whinnying to get in for her breakfast.

Lying on my side, listening to Poetry's squawky voice read, I was thinking about another mystery, which was: *What happened to Charlie Paxton, whose forearm I'd bitten and whose stomach I'd socked a fist into that exciting night?* I was just ready to ask if anybody knew, when Poetry went on.

"And here's another Rolling Stone from the *Avalanche.* 'Charlie Paxton has undergone psychiatric examination at the State Hospital and seems to be completely normal. He's had what the doctors call a *catharsis,* his fear of having caused Connie's death is gone, and he is well.'"

I rolled over and sat up when Poetry read that, because I'm going to be a doctor someday, and any medical term I'd never heard of always makes me want to know more about it.

And that is the story of the mystery of Wild

Horse Canyon. Maybe, as the *Avalanche* says, the rest of it will be solved someday. If it ever is, I'll probably write about it for you in another story about the Sugar Creek Gang.

All of a sudden, from beside me, Dragonfly let out a long-tailed sneeze, saying at the end of it, "Come on, gang, let's go in swimming! Last one in's a cow's tail!"

We all jumped up then, skinned ourselves out of our clothes, and started on a pell-mell dash for the creek.

SINCE 1894, Moody Publishers has been dedicated to equip and motivate people to advance the cause of Christ by publishing evangelical Christian literature and other media for all ages, around the world. Because we are a ministry of the Moody Bible Institute of Chicago, a portion of the proceeds from the sale of this book go to train the next generation of Christian leaders.

If we may serve you in any way in your spiritual journey toward understanding Christ and the Christian life, please contact us at www.moodypublishers.com.

> *"All Scripture is God-breathed and is useful for teaching, rebuking, correcting and training in righteousness, so that the man of God may be thoroughly equipped for every good work."*
> —2 TIMOTHY 3:16, 17